ArtScroll Youth Series®

Rabbi Nosson Scherman / Rabbi Meir Zlotowitz

General Editors

Published by
Mesorah Publications, ltd

Here, There, Every-where

Kids' true stories about finding Hashem in their lives

Avigail Sharer

FIRST EDITION
First Impression ... February 2012

Published and Distributed by
MESORAH PUBLICATIONS, LTD.
4401 Second Avenue / Brooklyn, N.Y 11232

Distributed in Europe by
LEHMANNS
Unit E, Viking Business Park
Rolling Mill Road
Jarow, Tyne & Wear, NE32 3DP
England

Distributed in Israel by
SIFRIATI / A. GITLER — BOOKS
6 Hayarkon Street
Bnei Brak 51127

Distributed in Australia and New Zealand
by **GOLDS WORLDS OF JUDAICA**
3-13 William Street
Balaclava, Melbourne 3183
Victoria, Australia

Distributed in South Africa by
KOLLEL BOOKSHOP
Ivy Common
105 William Road
Norwood 2192, Johannesburg, South Africa

ARTSCROLL YOUTH SERIES®
HERE, THERE, EVERYWHERE

ISBN 10: 1-4226-1179-5 / ISBN 13: 978-1-4226-1179-1

Typography by CompuScribe at ArtScroll Studios, Ltd.

Printed in the United States of America by Noble Book Press Corp.
Bound by Sefercraft, Quality Bookbinders, Ltd., Brooklyn N.Y. 11232

For my precious children
Michal Esther, Yehudis, Mordechai,
Yehoshua Leib, and Yosef Chaim

Contents

Acknowledgments

When this book was no more than the cusp of an idea, floating at the corner of my consciousness, I would walk down the street, mentally composing the acknowledgments.

Finally! A forum for thanks. The chance to say something meaningful and beautiful and appreciative and insightful and loving.

Six hours ago, Miriam Zakon called me. "Time for acknowledgments."

I sit in front of the computer, quailing at the task.

Because, when all is said and done, the words *thank you* are poverty stricken. They stretch forth, begging alms. Two paltry words. How can they express a writer's debt to an editor who has taken an idea and nurtured it into a book? A daughter's debt to a mother and father who stood beside me as I took my first ever steps and who stood beside me as I stepped up to the *chupah*, and who lend every day a painstakingly woven cushion of love and caring and security? A wife's debt to a husband who shares every minute and every tear — of sorrow and of joy and of yearning. A Jew's debt to her Creator, Who lovingly bestows gift upon gift upon gift, asking in return only those very two words: Thank You.

This, though, is all I have. And so this is what I offer.

To Esther Heller, without whose constant encouragement I would not be writing. And for a precious friendship.

Tzirel Strassman gave me my first chance at writing for children, in *Mishpacha Junior*. Along the way, she's become a mentor, adviser, and friend.

Rabbi Paysach Krohn's Tishah B'Av *derashah* on *Emunah* spurred me forward, and his enthusiastic endorsement of this book was a tremendous source of encouragement.

The volume of stories I received from the girls of Gateshead Jewish Primary School was staggering. Thank you to every single one of you for making so much effort. I enjoyed every story and I've kept them all — who knows, perhaps they'll make it into another volume.

To the ArtScroll team (in Israel) — it is a privilege to work with a company that measures each project by the impact it will have on *Klal Yisrael*. In particular, Reb Shmuel Blitz — it has been a pleasure to work with you. Miriam Zakon — thank you for a special friendship.

To the ArtScroll team (in New York) — I would like to express my appreciation for all that you have done to enhance my book. In particular, Mrs. Judi Dick for editing; Mrs. Mindy Stern for proofreading; Mrs. Estie Dicker for pagination; Devorah Bloch for the striking cover; and last but surely not least, Mendy Herzberg for bringing it all together with his usual efficiency and good cheer.

To my family — Ilana and Noam, Tania, Deborah and R' Emmanuel, Binyomin and Liora, Yehoshua and Elisheva, Boruch, and Aryeh. What a family we are! How blessed we are to always have each other. To my wonderful Sharer sisters- and brothers-in-law, in particular Judy and R' Dovid Reuven. To my nieces and nephews for their stories — especially Esti and Chani. And to Shoshana and Ruthie, my honorary sisters here in RBS.

To Deborah, for stories and ideas and *chizuk* and endless understanding. And for being the greatest sister!

To Daddy and Mummy Sharer for your loving support and for your constant eager inquiries: What's new with our wonderful grandchildren?

To Daddy and Mummy, for always believing in me and showing me how proud you are. And for your endless caring and love.

To Yitzchok, for implanting and imprinting the message of this book on my heart and soul.

Tov lehodos LaHashem ... Lehagid baboker chasdecha ve'emunascha baleilos.

Avigail Sharer
Cheshvan 5772

A Note to Parents

"Where is Hashem? I can't see Him!"

It's a question that's asked by every child.

When my children asked me that question I took them to the window and opened it wide. We looked at the trees, the flowers, the blue sky, and the fluffy white clouds. "Close your eyes," I told them. Three little faces screwed up their eyes obediently. "What can you feel?" I said.

"Feel?"

"Yes. Keep still for a moment and feel."

"I feel the wind," my little one piped up.

"And can you see that wind?"

The three of them giggled. "Of course not, Mommy!"

"Can you see the wind when you open your eyes?"

"No!"

I closed the window and led them to the couch. "Just like you can't see the wind, although it's right there, you can't see Hashem. You can feel Him though, all the time, because He's right here, in this room, along with us."

It might be the most important lesson our parents ever teach us, and the most important lesson that we can, in turn, impart to our own children. It's the key to a personal, loving relationship with our Creator. Hashem's here. He loves us and cares for us and takes care of us every moment of every day.

When we internalize this lesson — and it's a lifetime's work — every aspect of our humdrum lives is transformed. Our davening becomes a conversation with He Who understands us and wants the best for us; our mitzvos become part of an ongoing dialogue with Hashem. Our days become infused with the joy born of the knowledge that our actions count, that our lives make a difference.

How can we achieve this lofty goal? It is said that R' Chatzkel Levenstein (*Mashgiach* in Mir and Ponovezh), one of the great *mussar* personalities of the previous generation, would reward his children with candies every time they told him a story of *hashgachah pratis*, each time they opened their eyes and recognized Hashem's involvement in their day-to-day schedules.

Here, There, Everywhere is aimed at giving parents and children a jump-start. Reading of how other children opened their eyes can be the springboard and example for our children to copy. These are all true stories — some are remarkable and some more mundane. Because whether it's finding a lost sticker album or finding a long-lost father, the lesson is there. Hashem is right here: we just have to open our eyes and see Him.

A Note to the Reader

The branches scratch your cheeks and the night air is filled with the sound of leaves rustling underfoot and the crack of snapping twigs. You look up, but the trees block your vision. A full moon shines down, but you can't see it. You can't see anything.

You are lost. And it's dark.

And then you find a lantern, a dim candle glowing in a glass case. The flame flickers and dances and your heart lifts. Perhaps you will find the path you seek. Perhaps you can make it until the morning sun breaks through the darkness.

We all go through hard times, times when we're in pain, when there's an ache inside. The sun may be shining, but we feel the night pressing in on us. We need a lantern. We need an encouraging light that will warm us and give us hope.

That light is Hashem.

Hashem is with us. He's guiding us. He loves us. He is our lantern. When we hold on to Him, we feel that encouraging glow.

If the darkness seems to be closing in on us, all we need to do is to open our eyes.

The children in these stories come from all over the world: South Africa, Israel, America, England. They are different from one another, they like different foods, they think differently. There's one thing they have in common: they all opened their eyes to see Hashem's light in their lives. To see His "*hashgachah pratis*," His special care for what happens to each of us.

I'm sure there are times when you, too, felt the hand of Hashem close by. I'd love to hear about it.

Please, be in touch: hashgachahpratis1@gmail.com.

Avigail

Orangutans and Oranges

I was concentrating on stopping the spaghetti slide through my fork when Mommy made the announcement. This year, she said, we would be staying home for summer vacation. I heard my fork clatter onto the table. Horrified, I looked up at her. "What?" I said. "No vacation?"

"I didn't say *no vacation*," Mommy corrected me. "I said no *away* vacation. But we'll still have vacation at home. You'll see, we'll do loads of fun things — projects and scavenger hunts, and trips to different places. We can have picnics in the park, and maybe we'll go to the beach and have a barbecue and ..."

It turned out that Mommy's ideas really did sound like fun. By the time supper was over, the thought of staying home didn't seem quite so bad after all. Still, I was careful to keep a grumpy look on my face, just to make sure that this year's summer vacation would really be a special one.

And guess what? We really did have a good time. Maybe

even a great time. Each week, we took a grand trip. Okay, if Mommy made us write all about it afterward, we'd just roll our eyes and get to it. But the trip itself was something special.

That's how, one steamy summer day, we all ended up at the zoo. We paid, ran in through the turnstile, and, to keep my brother Yossi happy, headed straight for the lions. The lions didn't like the heat too much; they just lay there, sunbathing. Occasionally, one of them opened his mouth in a gigantic yawn, which we all tried to copy. I did, too, even though it hurt my jaw.

We'd brought along loads of drinks, and we stopped and bought ices as well. The heat was making Mommy a bit tense. Every time she saw Yossi take off his baseball cap, she stopped and wouldn't continue until he put it back on. "But it makes me so hot! And sweaty!" he complained.

"I know it does. But I can't have the sun beating down on you like this. You'll get sick, *chas v'shalom*."

Yossi put the cap back on, but as soon as Mommy looked away, he took it off again. When she wasn't waiting for Yossi, Mommy had to keep dashing after little Naftali, who had just figured out how to unfasten the straps of his stroller and kept running off. Mommy's cheeks were red and she kept wiping her forehead with the back of her hand.

The only ones who seemed to be cool and calm were the elephants: they kept going back into the water and spraying it over their backs and legs. The penguins were okay, too. But the camels just lay there in the dust, and even the monkeys seemed too hot to do any jumping around. The orangutans were okay, as well, and Naftali kept pointing up at them. "Owandz," he repeated. "Owandz."

They really did look like oranges, high up in those trees. Not one that I'd want to taste, though.

Despite it all — and despite the peacock that shrieked into

Yossi's ear as he bit into his sandwich (he almost burst into tears, but just managed to stop himself; he's not as tough as he makes out) — we had a great time. We stayed until the bell rang through the huge zoo and announcements over the loudspeaker told us that there was only 10 minutes to closing time. I looked around and saw that there were hardly any visitors left. There were a few workers carrying large buckets, hurrying from the enclosures, but the visitors were gone and the stores were closed.

It's a big zoo, and it took us time to reach the large iron gates of the exit. All the time, my sister Shuli was whining: "I'm thirsty! I want a drink!" Mommy shook her head and told Shuli that the last thing she needed was to be locked inside the zoo for the night, and that Shuli would just have to wait till we got to the car. "It won't be long now," she said as she strode toward the exit, with Naftali in the stroller and us kids running behind.

We waved goodbye to the zookeepers and stepped outside. "Please, Mommy, *now* can I have a drink?" Shuli pleaded.

Mommy took a deep breath and pushed down the brake on the stroller. "No problem."

There was one more bottle of water. When we had set out that morning, it had been a block of ice. The ice had melted by now, and the water was warm. But at least there was plenty for everyone.

Just as Mommy unscrewed the cap, little Naftali decided that the time had come to make his escape. He clicked open the straps and wriggled out of his stroller. As fast as his pudgy legs would carry him, he ran off in the direction of the zoo gates. When he got there, he lay down on his tummy and crawled underneath so that he was inside the zoo. From the other side of the locked gates, he stood up and gave us all a cheery wave.

Mommy dropped the bottle of water to the ground and ran over. Reaching through the bars, she grabbed Naftali by the hand and held on, tight. "Help!" she called out. "Help!"

There was no answer.

"Can somebody, anybody help me?"

Everyone had gone home. There was no one to help.

She tried coaxing Naftali back under the gate. "Want a cookie?"

Naftali shook his head.

"A lollipop?"

Naftali shook his head.

"Ice cream?"

Naftali shook his head. "Owandz," he said, pointing. "Wan Owandz."

Mommy was starting to panic and Naftali looked like he might erupt in one of his super-screaming sessions. What should we do? Naftali was stuck inside the zoo, and we were stuck outside.

I had an idea.

"Mommy, call the zoo!"

Mommy's face brightened. "Great idea, Esty."

There was a phone number on the brochure and I carefully punched it into Mommy's cell phone. When a voice answered, I handed the phone to Mommy. She quickly explained what had happened and, within 5 or 10 minutes, a tall zookeeper with a huge set of keys appeared, ready to release Naftali from his prison. By now, Naftali's face was red and he looked tired and limp.

"Wadeh," he said, pointing to a cup. "Wan wadeh."

"Sure, Naftali, let's get you a drink," I said. But there was no water. The last bottle had spilled out on the sidewalk. Mommy searched through all the bags, but there was nothing. No water. No juice. No soda. No milk bottle. Nothing.

Mommy touched her hand to Naftali's forehead. "He's hot," she said, creasing her eyebrows in worry. "He might have sunstroke."

"But we're all thirsty," Shuli whined.

"All of us," Yossi repeated.

Mommy looked around, but by now it was late. All the stores were closed. The zookeeper who had freed Naftali had also disappeared.

"Why don't we just drive home real fast?" I said.

Mommy shook her head. "It's a two-hour drive, Esty. I can't leave him without fluid for two hours. He could get seriously ill, *chas v'shalom*."

"So what are we going to do?" Shuli wailed. She opened her mouth, about to launch into hysterics, but Mommy gave her a Look. She strapped Naftali into the stroller. He was too tired and hot to try to get out again. "We're going to head back to the car and see if we have any water there," Mommy told us.

It was a long walk to the car, and we walked as fast as we could. We opened the doors and searched under the seats for a bottle. Nothing. There was nothing in the trunk, either.

By now, Mommy was getting really worried. She kept feeling Naftali's red cheeks and hot forehead and pushing his blond curls away from his face. And that was when I saw it.

"Look, Mommy!"

A little way up the sidewalk was a man dressed all in orange, with a huge hat that was shaped like an orange. It looked really strange. A huge poster next to him was promoting Sunburst, a new brand of pure Florida orange juice. He was handing out small cartons for people to sample. I ran up to him and asked for a carton. He gave it to me. I thanked him and ran back to the car and gave it to Naftali. He drank it down greedily. Shuli and Yossi went over to the man and asked if he had any more spare cartons.

"I'm heading off home, now," he told us. "I've still got some samples left over. I'll gladly give them to you." He reached into his cooler box and took out an armful of cartons.

"Here you go," he said. "Tomorrow I'm stationed outside the theme park, 30 miles up the highway. I've never stood outside the zoo before. But it looks like I was at the right place at the right time."

We all nodded and smiled, but when we were back in the car, sipping cool orange juice we burst out like those Sunburst oranges, "Isn't it amazing, Mommy!"

"We were all so thirsty and now look!"

Mommy looked at us all through the rearview mirror. "It sure is amazing, kids. Just think, the same way Hashem makes the sun shine on those oranges in Florida, so they grow big and juicy for us to drink, He's taking care of us, too."

We were all nodding our heads and agreeing, when Naftali looked at the juicy orange and gave a grin. "Owandz."

Happy Birthday!

"I do *not* want to go to bar mitzvah lessons!" I yelled as I stomped upstairs and into my room, slamming the door behind me. I can't carry a tune, I hate talking to people I don't know, and the thought of standing up in synagogue in front of a whole room packed with strangers ... *And* I can barely read Hebrew. Any wonder that the thought of bar mitzvah lessons is a real drag?

Thing is, there's no one to moan to, no one who understands me, no one, no one, no one. Just me. Me myself and I. I don't have a brother and I don't even have a sister. Kids with brothers and sisters always tell me I'm so lucky — no one taking your stuff, no one grabbing all the attention ... But I say that it's boring and there's no one to play with. I've wanted a little brother or sister *forever* ... but here I am, still the only one in the family. And now I'm having this bar mitzvah and that's all my parents are thinking about. There's no sisters to take shopping and there's no brothers to tell off for traipsing mud through the house. Just me and this *haftarah* that I can't seem to learn.

Even though my family is not religious, they wanted this to be a proper bar mitzvah, so they set me up with this rabbi. Even though I didn't want to go.

Five-fifteen that Sunday afternoon had me knocking lightly on the thick wooden door of Rabbi Feigenbaum's house. Mrs. Feigenbaum opened the door with a big smile, and showed me inside. Feigenbaum sounds like a real, old Jewish name, right? Well, it fit the rabbi perfectly. He had white hair, a large black yarmulke, a face full of wrinkles, and eyes that crinkled. The only un-rabbi-like thing about him was that he didn't have a beard.

Mrs. Feigenbaum set down a plate of yeast cake — the kind that melts in your mouth and on your fingers too and then I had to lick the chocolate from my fingers and wonder if that was very rude. I was sure that Mom wouldn't like it.

Rabbi Feigenbaum just gave this throaty kind of chuckle. "There's nothing like my wife's kokosh," he said. He didn't want to hear a word about the *haftarah*. He told me that we would begin that four weeks before the big day. I wasn't sure how mom would feel about that; she likes things organized in advance [she'd already booked the hall and the caterer, and she was hunting for the perfect bar-mitzvah-mother hat — even though there was still a year to go]. Rabbi Feigenbaum wanted to do two things, he told me. He wanted to give me a taste of Jewish education, and he wanted to brush up my Hebrew reading.

The reading part was a bit excruciating, but it was over pretty quick and then we got onto the more interesting stuff.

"What's a bar mitzvah all about?" Rabbi Feigenbaum asked.

I shrugged. "A big birthday party?"

He shook his head. "I'll give you a hint. It's something to

do with the name: bar mitzvah. Mitzvah. Do you know what a mitzvah is?"

"Uh . . . like a good deed?" I had heard Dad say it to Mom sometimes, when someone new moved into the neighborhood and they invited them for dinner.

"That's part of the answer, but not the whole answer. A mitzvah is a command, given by G-d and written down in the Torah. There are 613 mitzvos, which include keeping Shabbos and kosher, putting on tefillin each day, not slandering or speaking badly about other people, visiting the sick, returning a lost item, and more."

I nodded. Sounded vaguely familiar.

"But that's not all. The word mitzvah contains within it another word: *tzavta*, which means to accompany. Mitzvos are the way in which we accompany G-d, so to speak. On the simplest level, that means that we do the things He wants us to do, and so we feel close to Him."

I'd never heard this stuff before and I listened carefully. "You mean G-d really cares about what I do?"

"Absolutely." He reached for a thick book, with a maroon and gold cover and opened it. Then he read a bunch of Hebrew words. "Now I'll translate: 'You are children of Hashem your G-d.' Does your Dad care about you and about what you do?"

I nodded. "For sure."

"Well, Hashem cares even more than your father. He's the One Who *gave* you a father and mother."

I looked at him.

"Think about it," Rabbi Feigenbaum said.

And I did.

Every week after that, Rabbi Feigenbaum chose one of the mitzvos and taught me about it. Mostly, he told good — no, great — stories about the mitzvah, and asked questions that I'd never thought of before. He never told me the answers, though. He told me to go away and think, and the next week we'd discuss what I thought and sometimes he'd offer a few thoughts of his own.

I'd had around six lessons when I suddenly realized that I was enjoying this stuff. Mom and Dad kept asking me how the *haftarah* was going, and asking why they didn't hear me practicing, but I explained that we were doing some preparatory stuff first, and they were okay with that. After all, even though Mom kept list after list in her iPad, the bar mitzvah wasn't for another ten months.

I asked Mom and Dad if we could up the lessons to two a week, and they were thrilled that the dreaded bar mitzvah lessons were a success. In the second session, Rabbi Feigenbaum taught me some Chumash and a little bit of Mishnah. Now that my Hebrew reading was improving, getting through the text wasn't as awful, and I caught on quickly to the three-letter root thing he showed me.

At the end of one lesson, Rabbi Feigenbaum brought out an oversized orange cup with two handles.

"This is a *negel vasser* cup," he said, and explained how to wash my hands in the morning. He gave me the cup as a gift, and I started using it every morning, the way he taught me. Three times on each hand, washing up to the wrist, as soon as I woke up.

A few weeks later, we started talking about Shabbat. Rabbi F gave me some books to read about it, and I stayed up late that night, long after Mom had wished me good night and turned off my bedroom light. I snuck out of bed, found my flashlight, and sat under the covers, reading all about the special day of Shabbat, about how it's a gift that G-d gave the Jews, about the candles and the two braided loaves of challah, and the sweet wine and the special feeling of peace and tranquility.

I *want that*. I found myself thinking. *I want to have Shabbat*.

But it would also be hard, I realized. No movies, no television, no computer games. No picking up the phone to arrange to meet a friend, no riding in the car and barbecuing in the park ... Could I really do it?

Late, late that night, I closed the book and, wrapping my quilt around me, I stood by my bedroom window. Outside, the sky was black and a new moon could be seen just above the trees.

I looked upward. "G-d," I whispered. "I'm going to try to keep Shabbat. But I want You to do something for me, too," I closed my eyes tight. "Please, G-d, please, give me a baby brother or sister. Please."

I thought for a minute. "And just to know that it's from You and this is all for real, make the baby be born on my birthday. Thank You."

After that conversation, I tried really hard to keep my word. The first Shabbat was easy; Rabbi Feigenbaum invited me to stay with him. I had to work real hard remembering not to flip the lights on or off, but when I got used to it, it was great. Shabbat afternoon, Rabbi Feigenbaum had arranged for a kid my age to pick me up and take me to his house to hang out. The kid's name was Pinchas, which was kind of hard for me to say, but he told me I could call him Pinny, and that worked. Pinny is Rabbi Feigenbaum's nephew, and he has a crazy sense of humor — kept me laughing that whole afternoon long. The next Shabbat, Pinny invited me to spend with him and his family and it was great. I was starting to feel like a pro.

Shabbat at home was more complicated. Mom and Dad didn't mind, they kept joking that I was going through my teenage rebellion a little earlier than most, but it was harmless enough. Mom even bought challahs at the kosher bakery and made a special meal, and we all enjoyed it — enough to do it the week after, and after that, too.

A few months later, my parents sat me down and told me that they had some good news for me. "How would you like a little brother or sister?"

"For real?"

"For real."

That night, I couldn't sleep. I wrapped my quilt around me and stared out of my bedroom window. The sky was black and a new moon could be seen just above the trees. "Thank You, G-d," I whispered. "Thank You."

The next few months passed quickly. Midterms and end of term exams and vacation plans and invitations and flower arrangements and shopping for a new suit and shoes. And . . . there was also a nursery to plan and decorate and baby clothes and blankets to buy.

The bar mitzvah finally rolled around and despite my nerves, I did Rabbi Feigenbaum and my parents proud. I said the *berachot*, chanted the *haftarah*, and even made a speech, thanking everyone for coming and my parents for making me such a nice bar mitzvah.

Eleven days later, my baby brother was born. I went to see him in the hospital and I was even allowed to hold him after I scrubbed my hands and cut my fingernails. Such tiny fingers, such smooth cheeks. I couldn't believe that a real life person was in that weeny baby.

I'd made up to continue my lessons with Rabbi Feigenbaum, even after the bar mitzvah. I didn't go for a couple of weeks after the bar mitzvah, what with the new baby and everything, and when I finally had a lesson, Rabbi Feigenbaum greeted me with a booming "Mazel tov!" We sat down to start learning. Before long, though, he sensed that something was troubling me. "What's on your mind, Sammy?" he asked.

I told him. I told him about my promise to G-d, and how I had asked that, in return, He send me a brother or sister.

I had kept my promise, I told Rabbi F, and G-d had indeed sent me what I had been longing for. But not on my birthday.

Rabbi Feigenbaum looked at me thoughtfully for a long while. "The baby was born two weeks ago, no?"

I nodded. "On a Wednesday."

"Wednesday night or Wednesday morning?"

"Morning."

Rabbi Feigenbaum reached for the calendar he kept on his desk and flipped two pages. "According to the Hebrew calendar, that's the eighteenth of Sivan," he said.

"Right," I said. "Not on my birthday."

"But when is your real birthday?" he asked. "You can't expect G-d to go according to the secular calendar."

I hadn't thought of that. Could it be?

"My English birthday's on May 12."

Rabbi Feigenbaum took a large, shiny, brown volume down from his book shelf. He flipped through the pages until he reached 1997, the year I was born. "In 1997, May 12th fell out on ..." He paused.

My heart skipped a beat.

"Eighteenth of Sivan."

Rabbi Feigenbaum pushed his glasses down his nose and peered at me with those blue eyes of his. "So, Sammy, what do you say?" he said. "Looks like Hashem gave you the birthday present you asked for, after all."

The Right Medicine

It's always tough when any of the kids are sick, you know what I mean? Dudi lies on the couch, moaning and groaning and complaining that the tea Mommy makes is too hot or too cold or too sweet or not sweet enough. Naftali isn't much better. Everyone gets grumpy. Even Mommy, 'cause she has to take time off work. And, as she always says, when we get sick, she's stuck in the house and what if we run out of milk or something? The only one who doesn't mind too much is Chani — 'cause she always gets tons of visitors and she loves it when she doesn't have school.

So this year, after Succos, when the weather started turning cold, I told myself that this winter, I'm not going to get sick. It worked for a few weeks, but ... I guess that bugs and germs don't always listen to 9-year-old boys, know what I mean?

The day my stomach started to flip-flop worse than the roller-coaster I went on in the summer, and I started to feel hotter than I did on August 7th, which was the hottest day this year, I knew that something was up. I had to sit down in the middle of davening, and I didn't even care that the rest of the kids were looking at me and wondering what was up. My head felt so heavy that it kind of drooped down on my arms all by itself. Some place in the distance, I heard Rebbi explaining a difficult Mishnah and Sruly, the class genius, answering all the questions. Suddenly, I felt a cool hand on my forehead. I looked up with just my eyes. Rebbi looked down at me, full of concern.

"Why Simcha, you're burning up!" he said. He asked Sruly to go fetch me a glass of water and sent Menachem to the school secretary with a note to call my mother. "I'm sending you home, young man," he said in his I-mean-business voice. "And I don't expect to see you here tomorrow, either."

I nodded, and closed my eyes again. When I opened them, my mother was standing next to me, my schoolbag slung over her shoulder. She helped me to my feet and led me to the car. Once we got home, she gave me some icky-tasting medicine to bring down the fever and tucked me up into bed.

"Let's hope it's just a 24-hour thing," she said as she tiptoed out. I could hear her putting a load of laundry in the dryer, then I heard her footsteps going down the stairs. The vacuum cleaner went on for a few minutes, and then I heard her talk some on the phone. After that, I must have fallen asleep, because the next thing I knew, Mommy was sitting beside me, sponging my face with a wet washcloth, and Chani was sitting next to her, moaning about a math quiz.

The next day, my fever still hadn't broken. "I'm calling the doctor," Mommy said. Somewhere in the distance, I heard my mother call in to work and tell them that she couldn't come in that day. I felt bad when I heard that, and I hoped I wasn't being a nuisance. But when Mommy came in later, she told me that she was only too glad to have a day off from work and I felt better. I fell asleep then, and only woke when the doctor was standing over me.

I like Dr. Fried. His hands always have a clean, doctorish kind of smell, know what I mean? He's always got a joke to tell me, and I smile, even when they're not too funny. When he peered down at me that day, he didn't look very jolly at all. He took a throat culture, which almost made me gag, and listened to my chest. "Doesn't seem to be anything wrong," he said, "but I don't like this fever. We'll keep a close eye on you."

The fever continued for two whole weeks. Dr. Fried had told Mommy to check my temperature three times a day and write it down. My friends kept calling and asking if they could visit, but I wasn't up to seeing anyone. Even my rebbi came over one day, after *cheder*. He came into my room, but my eyes were closed and he didn't want to disturb me. When Dudi told me he had come, I was so embarrassed. Imagine! Rebbi seeing me in my pajamas!

But Mommy wasn't happy and neither was Dr. Fried, although I was so sick that I didn't realize that they were so worried. They did blood tests and throat swabs and took me to a special clinic for X-rays ... and they still didn't know what was wrong.

"Enough is enough," said Dr. Fried, clapping his hands together. "I'm starting you on antibiotics. I don't know what for, but maybe there's an infection somewhere and the antibiotics will help. And if the fever hasn't broken in 24 hours, you're heading straight to the hospital."

I nodded, but I didn't say anything. I was very weak, y'see, and it was hard for me to even talk. I opened my mouth and swallowed the first dose of antibiotics. Not too long after that, I suddenly felt really nauseous. Mommy phoned Dr. Fried. "Let's switch antibiotics," he said, and he told Mommy that he would leave a prescription by the desk in his office. Mommy ran out in the car to pick it up.

As she poured the medicine into a spoon, she said a little *tefillah*, asking Hashem to make me better. "*Ribono shel Olam ... Yehei esek zeh le'refuah ki Rofeh chinam Atah.*" ["Master of the World, may this bring a complete recovery, for You are the Ultimate Healer."] I whispered Amen and swallowed the medicine. I laid my head back on my pillow and drifted into sleep. My mother woke me every four hours and dribbled a dose of medicine into my mouth, along with a sip of water. Sometime the next morning, I woke, feeling ... different.

I opened my eyes, looked out the window at the sun, shining through the trees. What was different? Suddenly, I knew. The cotton wool that had been stuffed inside my head had gone. My head felt normal.

"Moooommmmmmmy!" I yelled.

I put one foot over the side of my bed onto the floor. I thought that maybe I'd go downstairs for breakfast. When I stood up, though, I was very shaky and I flopped back into bed.

"Mooooommmmmmmyy!"

Mommy came running upstairs. She was still talking into the phone as she sat down beside me on the bed and placed a hand over my forehead. She looked very surprised to feel that I was cool. The fever had gone.

She sat there, nodding and hmmming into the phone, and a few minutes later she pressed Off and turned to me. "Simcha! You're looking better. Guess what?"

I shrugged my shoulders.

"That was Dr. Fried on the phone. Some more test results came back. We've found out what was wrong with you."

"What?" I said, happy that Chani wasn't here to make some mean comment about everything being wrong with me.

"Salmonella. That's a very serious form of food poisoning."

"Oh."

"But listen to the incredible *hashgachah pratis*: For some strange reason, you couldn't stomach the first type of antibiotics, remember?"

I sure did.

"The second type of medicine he gave you is much more unusual and expensive. But apparently, recent studies have shown it to be an effective medicine to treat Salmonella — the food poisoning that you had."

Mommy put her arm around my shoulders and gave me a squeeze. "Look, Simcha, it's working. Hashem made sure you got the medicine that you needed, even though we didn't know what was wrong with you."

After that, it took only a few days till I was up and walking around. And, believe it or not, a week later, I was even missing *cheder*. When I finally got back to class — after having been away for almost a month — I was greeted by a huge sign that my classmates had decorated for me:

Baruch Rofei Cholim
Thanks, Hashem, for making Simcha better

It was a thank You that I, too, meant with all my heart. Know what I mean?

On Strike!

Have you ever said or done something and right away wish you had a magic powder that could make you invisible? Oh, I'm Nosson, by the way. My family calls me Nossy and you can, too, if you like. I'm one of those kids who's always doing the kind of stuff that makes your cheeks go red and hot. Y'know, when you wish that you could press a secret button and push your words back into your mouth? Like the time when I got a piece of meat stuck in my teeth at my cousin's bar mitzvah. I always heard Mommy talking about choking, and how dangerous it is, and I thought that choking means something just getting stuck. So, when the meat was stuck I thought that I was choking. I ran up to my Tatty, who was standing at the front of the hall, giving a *derashah*. "Call an ambulance!" I yelled. The microphone picked up my voice and everyone around the hall heard me yell for an ambulance when all I needed was a toothpick. Talk about embarrassing.

Or there was the time when my pals were having a water fight in our front garden. It was boiling. Shmoiling. We turned on the sprinklers and raced through them and then I went inside and found some loot. Water pistols, *negel vasser* cups, bottles ... That's when things really started getting exciting. I snuck around the side of our house and filled up a huge bucket from the tap over there. Somehow, I managed to lift it. All the while, my friend Bentzy was calling me names, just asking for me to get him. I ran after him and he backed away, toward the street. One! Two! Three! Splash! I threw that water toward Bentzy but Bentzy sidestepped just in time. What I didn't realize, though, was that just at that moment, our rebbi was walking down the street. I threw the water; rebbi walked past. *Splash!* Rebbi was soaked, from his hat down to his shoes ...

The other day another embarrassing thing happened to me. I was sitting in class and instead of concentrating on fractions, I had my *siddur* on my lap and I was flipping through it. There's so much in there – *Moaz Tzur*, and *Hallel*, and *Shoshanas Yaakov*. There's also all the songs in *Hallel*, and in *Birchos Kerias Shema* ... there's music all over the place. I turned a few pages, and there was the Haggadah, which made me think about Pesach, and then I turned a few pages more and there was the song *Bar Yochai*, that we sing on Lag BaOmer. I was looking at it, reading the words, and, without even realizing it, I started tapping my feet to the song I was singing in my head. I started thinking about Meiron, of bonfires and roasted marshmallows and haircuts. I really wasn't in the classroom at all. I began tapping the beat on my desk and then I reached the chorus again. This time, instead of singing the words in my head, I opened my mouth and, loud and clear, sang, "*Bar Yochai, nimshachta ashrecha* ..."

Well, we were meant to be learning how to multiply fractions and the teacher wasn't too pleased, although the boys in my class had a good laugh, which made me feel dumb. I quickly closed my *siddur*, kissed it, and took a look at the problems in the textbook, hoping that everyone would forget about my solo.

The song didn't go away, though. I kept thinking about Meiron and little Chaim'ke, who's turning 3 just after Pesach. In our living room there are pictures of all of us boys in Meiron for our haircuts. It's one of those things that our family just does. With Chaim'ke, though, I wondered.

When I got home later that day, I asked Mommy if we would still go to Meiron this year with Chaim'ke. She sighed. "That's pretty far away, Nossy," she said. "How about we get through Succos first?"

She had a point, but I wasn't happy that the answer wasn't, "Yes! Of course! What's the question?"

But I guess that things are different now. You see, not so many months ago, my Tatty moved out of our house. Now he lives in a little apartment by himself and we see him every second Shabbos and once a week for pizza. I never thought you could get bored of pizza, but you can. And also of the takeout chicken that he buys for Shabbos when we go over. But most of all I just feel sad that we're not a real family anymore, that Tatty doesn't live with us.

For Succos, Mommy's brother, Uncle Nechemia, is coming to stay, along with his wife Auntie Mina, who is also Mommy's best friend in the whole world. They talk to each other almost every day. Uncle Nechemia is always telling funny jokes, and then he bursts out laughing as if he didn't know the punch line all along. He also knows fun places to go on trips. So it looks like it will be a good Succos, after all, even though I'll miss Tatty. We will see him of course, but you know what I mean.

Succos was ... well ... different. Like I said, Uncle Nechemia is loads of fun, and Auntie Mina is a mean cook — she makes *holishkes* that are so good you don't even know you're eating cabbage. We also visited Tatty and I felt bad when he took us into his little succah. It wasn't nice and sturdy like the one we have at home. It was made from plastic sheets, which flapped around a lot, and there was a mat of bamboo on the roof instead of the thick layer of green leaves that we always trim from the laurel bush in the garden. I think the bit that made me saddest was the decorations. Tatty had tied one silver chain across the top and he'd used safety pins to put up a poster of the Kosel. "Next year, I'll come and help you decorate it," I told him. Tatty just gave a funny smile.

Soon enough, Succos was over. I helped Uncle Nechemia pack away the succah while Auntie Mina was getting all their stuff together. They had a flight home the very next afternoon. We were taking down the large, fluorescent light when Auntie Mina came outside, talking so fast I couldn't understand what she was saying. Neither could Uncle Nechemia.

"Whoa, slow down, Mina. What're you saying?"

"It's just like I said. I told you — it was on the news and Ma's been telling me this all the time. There's a strike in the airport. There are no flights out. I don't know until when, even. All I know is that we're stuck. What's going to be?"

Uncle Nechemia carefully put down the light and followed Mina inside. They phoned the airport but they couldn't get through. They called the travel agent.

"I need to be home, you see!" Uncle Nechemia said into the phone. "I have an urgent meeting at work on Wednesday. There's no way I can miss it."

I wiggled my eyebrows to show Auntie Mina that I didn't understand why it was all such a crisis. I mean, what was the big deal if they stayed a few more days? Maybe we'd even get in the trip to the ice-cream store that they'd promised but we hadn't had any time for.

Mommy motioned me to come to the kitchen. "Nechemia has a very important business meeting on Wednesday," she explained. "Someone is flying in from Japan to talk to him."

"Oh." That explained it.

"Please don't disturb them while they're figuring out what to do, 'kay?"

I nodded and headed back outside to see which wall I should tackle next, and wondering whether I could manage without Uncle Nechemia to help me.

Meanwhile, in the living room, Uncle Nechemia had decided that there was no way he was missing this meeting. I could see him, pacing up and down the room, waving his arms around, as he made plans with the travel agent.

Eventually, he finished the call and I went inside to see what was happening. Turned out that some companies were still flying, and he'd gotten the most roundabout crazy ticket that left in five hours' time but that would get him home for the business meeting. Auntie Mina would stay on with us until El Al stopped the strike and she could use her regular ticket to get home.

So that's what happened. Uncle Nechemia took three connecting flights and got home in time, and Auntie Mina stayed with us for an extra six days.

When they got home and got over the jet lag, Uncle Nechemia wrote a letter to El Al, complaining about what had happened. They replied that they were processing his complaint and he should have patience until they got back to him.

I thought that it was pretty rude to tell a grownup to have patience, but since when did anyone listen to me . . .

After that, everything kind of got back to normal. Yeshivah, riding my bike, visiting Tatty. I even got used to making Kiddush for the family on Friday nights. Not that I like it much, but still.

Chaim'ke was getting bigger, too. His hair wasn't really curly and wasn't really straight. It kind of stuck up around his face like a big ball of brown fuzz. He was excited to have it cut. He kept saying in his cute little voice, "Chaim'ke have haircut. Get *tzitzis*. Get *peyos*. Get glasses." I thought that was so funny. I wear glasses and so does Motty, who's 7, and we just bought glasses for Dudi, even though he's only just 5, so Chaim'ke thought that he'd get glasses, too, at his *upsheren*. Told you he's a cute kid.

I figured it was about time to ask Mommy again about what we would do. "Nosson," she said gently, "things are different now. Even if we were to go to Meiron, who would cut Chaim'ke's hair?"

Tatty could, I was about to say, but I stopped myself. I didn't want to upset Mommy, but I was upset. For my *upsheren* and for Motty's and Dudi's we'd gone to Meiron. We still look at the photos each Lag BaOmer. And nobody believes me, because they think I was too young, but I'm telling you that I still remember it: the humongous bonfire, the dancing, the singing. It wasn't fair that Chaim'ke wouldn't have that. It just wasn't fair.

Next time I visited Tatty, I asked if he could take us to Meiron for Chaim'ke's *upsheren*. He gave me a funny smile — his lips curled up but his eyes didn't crinkle. He told me that it's just not possible and he doesn't want to talk about it any more.

Boy was I upset. Wasn't it bad enough that we weren't a regular family anymore? Why did Chaim'ke have to miss out on his special day?

The next day, I had an idea. I decided to write a letter. A real letter, with a stamp and everything, and send it to Uncle Nechemia. That night, after yeshivah, I tore a page from a loose-leaf, chewed my pen a couple of times and started writing. I told him how I was so upset and that it wasn't fair that Chaim'ke would miss out and how things were just plain hard sometimes without Tatty at home.

I looked up the address in the black phone book and sent it off that night. I forgot about the letter pretty soon: everyone was getting busy preparing for Purim and Mommy was busy worrying about Pesach and no one was thinking about how Chaim'ke was getting bigger and his hair was getting longer and in just a couple months' time he would be 3.

Boy was I surprised when I got a letter back in the mail. Mommy handed it to me one morning when I was eating my cornflakes. I ran up to my bedroom and tore open the envelope. It was from Uncle Nechemia.

Dear Nosson,

Hey, kid. How's it going? Whatcha doing on Purim?

Thanks for writing. You should do it more often — and not only when you're worried.

About the upsheren, me and Auntie Mina are trying to think of a solution. I'll keep you posted.

Say hi to everyone from me.

Uncle Nechemia

I was still reading when I heard Motty banging on my door. "Nossy, what's up? Who's that letter from, anyway?"

"Private property," I told him. I'd probably tell him about it later, but not now, with him bugging me. I lifted the side of my mattress and put the letter underneath just to be sure that no one would find it. Then I grabbed my schoolbag and ran out the front door, calling goodbye to Mommy before I closed the door. Phew. Didn't want to be late.

A few days later, Mommy mentioned that she had been talking to Auntie Mina. Well, that's nothing new, they talk almost every day. She said that Auntie Mina had been looking into tickets to come for Lag BaOmer, but everything was very expensive. That Japanese guy hadn't been such a great customer after all, and they didn't think it would work out.

"Oh," I said, nodding and pretending that I didn't mind at all.

But really, I did mind. A lot.

Purim was fun, Pesach was ... well, okay I guess. Now there were twenty days left until Lag BaOmer, Chaim'ke's big day. Every evening after Maariv I counted *sefirah*: *hayom shishah-asar yom sheheim shnei shavuos ushnei yamim ba'omer ...*

Hayom shivah-asar yom ...

Hayom shemonah-asar yom ...

Mommy started making honey cookies and freezing them, and I kinda realized that we weren't going to go to Meiron that year, after all.

That night, we were eating a yummy supper of burgers and chips when the phone rang. It's usually someone from America when the phone rings that time of day, so Mommy ran to answer it.

"Nechemia, how are you?"

I looked up.

Mommy went off into the living room to talk and she didn't say much but "Mmm" and "Hmmm" and "I see." Which didn't help me figure out what she was talking about at all.

A few minutes later, she came back into the kitchen and handed me the phone.

"Nossy!" Uncle Nechemia kind of yelled in a good kind of way down the phone.

"Hi, Uncle Nechemia!"

"Guess what?"

"What?"

"I just got a letter in the mail. Guess who it's from?"

How was I supposed to know? "Uh, don't know."

"It's from El Al. They finally got around to processing my complaint from Succos. Not only are they refunding me the money I spent getting home, but they're giving me a whole new ticket — for free!"

"Wow, that's great."

"So, then, can you start getting things ready?"

"Huh?"

"We're going to need scissors, a change of clothing, the camera, your Mommy's famous honey cookies ..."

"Do you ..."

"Yup, that's exactly what I mean. We're off to Meiron for the *upsheren*! How does that sound?"

All of a sudden it felt like a vacuum cleaner had come and sucked my voice away so I couldn't say anything, just a weird kind of croak. After a few minutes I tried again. "That sounds just great. Really, really great."

Chaim'ke didn't get glasses, but he looked great with his frizzy *peyos* and his short hair. There, on top of Mount Meiron, we gave him his *upsheren* and we sang and danced and stared at the huge fire that was taller than a house. Uncle Nechemia put his arms around us and together we all sang, "*Bar Yochai nimshachta ashreicha ...* "

Someone snapped a picture. When we got home, I developed it and I put it up next to my bed. I look at it and think about that night and how special it was. It gives me a good feeling inside. Sometimes I even wonder ... if I hold up my hands to the picture, will I still be able to feel the warmth of the fire on my fingertips?

Finding a Diamond

It's not fun living far away from Bubby and Zeidy but at least they come and visit us pretty often. My friend Suri has a Saba and Savta and they live in Eretz Yisrael. Last Succos they went to visit, but they haven't seen them since. I feel bad for her. When Bubby and Zeidy come there's such excitement.

This morning, as I walked into the kitchen to make sandwiches for school, Mommy gave me the good news: Bubby and Zeidy were coming for Shabbos! Yippee!

"You know, Mommy, last time they came, they slept in Shmuly's room, but I think that this time I'll move in with the baby and they should sleep in my bedroom."

"You think?"

"For sure. I want everything to be just perfect for them and my pink paint is so much prettier than those awful racing cars Shmuly has on his walls."

Mommy spread some peanut butter onto a slice of bread

and thought for a moment. "It's very kind of you, Rikki, but your bedroom isn't quite as large as Shmuly's."

"It would be okay if I moved my beanbag and my teddy collection."

Mommy wrapped up the sandwich and took the cottage cheese from the fridge to start on the next one. "Maybe. We'll have to think about it."

I looked at Mommy closely. She didn't seem so happy and I noticed that her eyes were pink. "Is anything wrong?" I asked.

Mommy gave a sigh. "It's just ... when I went to put my rings on this morning, I noticed that the diamond from my engagement ring had fallen out of the setting. I looked on the floor, in the drawer, in my jewelry box — but I couldn't find it. It's gone."

"Oh no!"

"I gave some money to *tzedakah*, but ... I can't believe that I'm going to find it. A diamond is so small ... Well, it should be a *kaparah*. A pretty big one." She paused. "Rikki, don't mention this to Bubby and Zeidy, will you? I don't want to upset them."

Mommy finished making the sandwiches and wiped down the counter. I stood there, watching her, not so sure of what to say. I knew that she was very upset. Diamonds cost a lot of money and Mommy always used to twirl her ring around her finger, watching how it caught the sunshine and sparkled like a star.

I felt bad for Mommy and I promised her that I would check the sidewalk on the way to school, just in case it had fallen out on the street. I looked carefully as I walked to school that morning, keeping my eyes on the gray stones as I went. I was concentrating so hard that I didn't even see my best friend Yocheved cross the street to join me, until she tapped me on the back and made me jump in surprise. I asked her to look at the left side of the sidewalk, and I looked at the right, in the hope that together, we'd find the diamond. But we only saw a few empty Coke cans and a lot of fallen leaves.

By the time I got home that afternoon, Mommy wasn't thinking about the diamond anymore. She was chewing the top of her pen as she wrote a shopping list, writing down all the things that Bubby and Zeidy like to eat on Shabbos.

"I must make carrot salad," she said. Shmuly wrinkled his nose. "I know that you kids don't like it, but it's Bubby's favorite." Mommy added carrots, Craisins, pineapple, and lemon juice to her list.

"Mommy, did you decide where Bubby and Zeidy will be sleeping?" I asked.

"As long as it's okay with Shmuly if they sleep in your bedroom, it's okay with me, too. But you'd better clean it up."

Shmuly said it was okay, so I took a box of oatmeal cookies up to my bedroom and told Sarale and Rutie that I would tell them a story while they tidied the room and put my teddy bear collection into a bag and shlepped it into the baby's room, where I'd be sleeping for Shabbos. They did a great job, so I handed out cookies and got them started making welcome signs for the front door.

The next day was Thursday. Mommy did the shopping on the way home from work, and then she went straight to the kitchen to start cooking. When I opened the front door after school that afternoon, there was a delicious smell of potato kugel. It made my mouth water. Mommy was busy peeling and chopping and the baby was in the highchair, banging the tray with his spoon. Mommy pointed to a bunch of yellow daffodils on the kitchen table. "Would you put them in a vase for me, Rikki?"

"Sure."

I climbed up to where the vases were kept and chose a pretty green one that would look nice on the desk in my bedroom. *If only we had a matching tablecloth*, I thought to myself. *Maybe I should call up Yocheved and see if they have one that we could borrow.*

I was thinking about that when the phone rang. I picked it up, said hello, and handed it to Mommy. It sounded like Sonya, the cleaning lady. She comes twice a week, on Monday and Thursday, and when I come home from school on those days there's a yummy fresh lemony smell. in the house.

Sure enough, Mommy started talking extra loud, the way she always does when she talks to Sonya. She's from Poland, you see, and she doesn't understand English too well. "But Sonya," she said, "I need you!"

After a few minutes, Mommy put the phone down. She looked upset.

"That was Sonya. She says she can't come. She's sick. We'll have to do all the cleaning ourselves. And Bubby and Zeidy are arriving tonight! You know how they like the house to be nice and neat."

"Oh, no!" I said.

"Yes. And I've been neglecting the housework so that I could concentrate on making Bubby and Zeidy's favorite dishes."

"I'll help, Mommy. I'm pretty good at cleaning and stuff."

"Thanks, Rikki." Mommy gave my cheek a stroke. "Who needs a diamond when you're around? Do you think you can start vacuuming upstairs for me?"

"Sure."

Mommy schlepped the vacuum cleaner up the stairs and plugged it in and I turned it on. I started in the hallway, trying hard not to miss any bits. Then I did my bedroom, all around the beds and behind the night table. I even stuck the nozzle under my bed to make it extra specially clean. But then one of my favorite hair clips got sucked up and I had to turn it off and ask Mommy to open the vacuum cleaner and look through all the dust to find it. After that I decided not to vacuum under the bed; Bubby and Zeidy wouldn't really notice anyway, especially now that Bubby has those special glasses with a line across the middle.

I vacuumed the kids' room, shooing them all up onto the top bunk so that I didn't have to vacuum around their feet, then Mommy told me to go and vacuum in her bedroom. I knocked lightly and went inside. By now, the top of my arm was starting to ache, so first I pushed the vacuum cleaner around real slow. Then I decided that the faster I do it, the faster I would be done. I took a deep breath, ready to go zooming around the room and cleaning it all super fast, when I noticed something. There was something small, sparkling in the carpet next to Mommy's bed. I walked closer and bent down, so that my nose was almost touching the floor. There, in the carpet, was Mommy's diamond.

I picked it up carefully and put it on the palm of my hand. It rolled a little, flashing all kinds of colors as it caught the light. Then I cupped my other hand over it and ran down the stairs.

"Mommmmmmmyyyyyy!"

"Rikki, please don't yell like that," came Mommy's voice from the kitchen.

I ran into the kitchen. "But look what I found!"

Mommy washed the challah dough from her hands and, shaking them dry, came to see why I was so excited. I opened my hands. Mommy gasped.

"Wow, Rikki. I can't believe it. My diamond!"

She picked it up carefully and blew off the dust. "You're a star! Where was it?"

"Next to your bed, on the carpet."

"*Baruch Hashem*," Mommy said and she started up the stairs to put the diamond safely away. "Rikki, imagine if the cleaning lady had come. She wouldn't have looked carefully like you did and that diamond would have been sucked into the dust bag and then emptied into the trash. Amazing."

She opened her jewelry box and put the diamond safely inside. "On Monday, I'll take it to the jeweler. In the meantime ..."

"The challah, right?"

"Right."

I ran down the stairs after Mommy and rolled up my sleeves. The dough was waiting. Bubby and Zeidy were coming, you see, and we wanted everything to be just perfect.

Lost and Found

I picked up my pajamas and stuffed them into the hamper. The chart on my bedroom wall was almost full. I just needed to pull the blanket neatly over my bed and ...

"Mommy!" I called, "I'm done."

Mommy looked around my bedroom with a smile. "Great job, Huvi." She reached into the pocket of her apron and pulled out a package of stickers. I chose a big, shiny silver one and stuck it on the last square of the chart. There! A whole month's effort and my cleanup chart was complete.

"We'll go get your prize this afternoon," Mommy said as she headed downstairs to remind the boys that the schoolbus was leaving in 6 minutes and if they didn't scoot ...

School that day dragged. It was hard to think about history or multiplication tables. I knew I was supposed to be looking at the pictures of birds that migrate in the fall but all I could see were rows and rows of stickers: stickers that glitter, stickers that smell, stickers that glow in the dark, stickers with tiny balls and bells, stickers that change picture when you tilt the angle. How many packages would Mommy let me choose, I wondered. And she had promised me a new sticker album, too.

School was finally over for the day and as soon as I got home, I asked Mommy when we could go to the store. "Catch your breath, first, sweetie," she said, patting my cheek.

"Okay!" I put my schoolbag in my room and went downstairs to wait.

When we finally got to the store, I didn't know what to choose. There was a whole wall covered, from the floor to the ceiling, with packages of stickers. The colors, the pictures, the miniature sticker photo frames . . . I stood and stared and stared. Until my older sister Adina gave me a shove and told me to get on with it. I looked carefully at each and every package, and, like Mommy told me, put aside my favorite. When I had finished looking, I had nine favorites to choose from. I went through them again, until I was left with two packages that I really loved. Mommy thought for a minute and then told me that she would buy both packages for me. Hurray! I was so excited to show them to Rifki and Chani in school the next day.

We paid and left the store, but by that time it was already dark. My younger brothers Eli and Pinny were saying that they were hungry. They said it over and over, so many times that Mommy decided to make a stop in the supermarket and pick up something for them to eat on the way home.

We followed Mommy into the store. The other kids were holding hands like Mommy said, but I was holding the pink bag containing my stickers and my new album. Mommy grabbed a bag of rolls, a ten-pack of chips, and stopped by the huge fridge to grab some yogurts. Then she remembered that we were out of apple juice, so we all went running off to the drinks department, stopping by the freezer section to get some pareve schnitzels. Three cartons of juice went into the cart, along with some soda for Shabbos. By the time we got to the checkout, Eli was crying and Pinny had knocked over a huge tower of toilet paper. The falling packages had bumped a worker on the head and Mommy made Pinny say sorry. That made Pinny even more wacky. He kept saying that it was an accident, so why did he need to apologize? Outside, it had started raining, and Adina was moaning that we hadn't brought our coats along and that she would get wet and her hair would get all curly.

I looked at Mommy as she unloaded the food onto the conveyer belt. She had a funny smile on her face. I wanted to try and help out, so I took a bag and started filling it with the cartons of juice.

We finally headed out the store with all the shopping. The bag I was carrying was heavy — I could feel it pressing against my palm. I was happy when we got to the car and I could hand it to Adina to dump in the trunk. Mommy settled everyone in the car and handed out bags of chips. Phew! Everyone stopped moaning and started munching. And that's when I noticed it.

"My stickers!" I pulled against the seat belt and felt the seat beneath me. Nothing. I looked in the shopping bags that were by my feet to see if my stickers were sitting under the yogurts. Nothing.

"Mommy!" I wailed. "My stickers."

Mommy gave a long sigh. "Have you checked all around you?"

I nodded.

"What about on the floor of the car?"

"I looked in the bags."

"Now look under and around the bags."

I peered down. It was hard to see in the dark, but I was pretty sure that nothing was there.

Mommy was quiet for a long time. At last she said, "All right, then. Everybody out."

We all piled out of the car and went right back into that store. I tried my best not to cry, even though it was hard.

We walked up and down the aisles, looking between the ketchup bottles and salad dressings and cans of corn and tuna. We looked at the towers of soda and bottled water. We even checked along the floor of the meat department, just in case my stickers and album had been kicked in that direction. Nothing. They were nowhere to be found.

The lady at Customer Services wasn't too helpful, either. While Mommy was talking, she kept telling her to hold on while she picked up the phone or made another announcement. I felt like waving my hands in front of her face to get her to listen. She took down our name and phone number and said that if someone turned in a pink bag with an album and two packages of stickers, she would get back to us.

We went around the store one more time. As I looked, I whispered the *perek* of Tehillim that we say after davening every day. I know it by heart. Then, Mommy turned to me. Her voice was very quiet. "It's very late, Huvi. Do you think we can head back home?"

I nodded my head. I think that if I had tried to say something, I would have just started to cry.

I kept quiet all the way home, and although I didn't look up to meet her eye, I could feel Mommy glancing up at me through the car mirror. By the time we pulled up outside our apartment block, Mommy was already telling the boys. "Sandwiches, pajamas, and bed, okay kids?"

But I wasn't in the mood of a sandwich. I wasn't in the mood of anything just then.

We pulled up and got out of the car just as Mrs. Schindler, one of our neighbors, was closing the outside door of the apartment block.

"Where are you going, Mrs. Schindler?" asked Pinny.

Mommy shushed him. She hates it when we ask our neighbors questions like that. Mrs. Schindler didn't seem to mind, though.

"I'm just off to the supermarket, kids."

"Oh," said Pinny. "Then look out for Huvi's stickers and album: she lost them while we were in the store."

Mrs. Schindler winked at Mommy. "I'll be sure to," she said, as she hurried toward the bus stop.

By the time everyone gulped down their tuna sandwiches, Eli had stopped being sleepy and was jumping around again. Mommy decided not to skip baths, after all. It took quite a while until we were all finally in bed. I tried to sleep, but all I could think of was how I had worked so hard to keep my room neat and clean — for a whole, entire month. What did I have to show for it? My beautiful stickers and my new album were lost, never to be found. I was very sad.

I was still staring at the dark ceiling when I heard the bedroom door open and then the clip-clop of Mommy's slippers. Mommy sat down on the bed next to me and stroked my hair. I sat up.

"Are you okay, Huvi?"

I nodded.

"Well, if you're not sleeping, there's someone here who wants to see you."

Me? To see me? I wondered who it could be.

Mommy gave me my robe to put over my pajamas and I followed Mommy to the front door. There, looking cold and wet, stood Mrs. Schindler. When she saw me, she bent down to my height and looked into my eyes. "I was just in the store, Huvi, and guess what I saw hidden in the fridge section?"

My heart started to beat fast. She pulled out a pink bag. "Is this what you were looking for?"

I took the bag and opened it. Yes! Inside was my album and my new stickers!

"When I saw the bag, sitting there among the yogurts, I picked it up and took it to Customer Services. They looked inside, and then they showed me the phone number you had left them. I recognized it of course, and I told them that I'd deliver the stickers and the album in person, right to the door."

"Thank you," I whispered.

Mrs. Schindler stood up and turned to Mommy. "Isn't it amazing that we met just that moment, as I was off to the store?"

"And that Pinny told you what had happened," Mommy added.

"And that I happened to notice the bag among all the stuff in that fridge," said Mrs. Schindler.

I went back to bed holding my stickers tight. I couldn't wait to show them to Rifki and Chani — and to tell them the amazing story of my stickers.

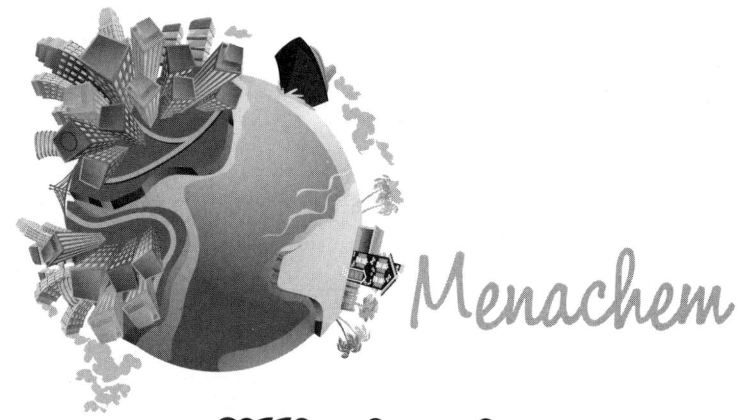

Tefillin in Time

"So, how are my son's tefillin getting on?" my father bellowed down the phone, a huge grin stretching across his face.

"His tefillin?" Maybe because the line wasn't too clear, or maybe because we were speaking English to an Israeli *sofer* — but it seemed that the *sofer* sounded a little confused.

"Of course, of course. I ordered tefillin from you. My Menachem's bar mitzvah is in less than three months. *Nu*, how's it going?"

"Three months? I didn't realize." Even though I was standing next to my father, and I didn't have the phone pressed hard against my ear like Tatty, I could still hear the *sofer* make a noise that sounded like a cross between a hiccup and a gulp. There was a pause and eventually he said, "You know what, call me in a week. I'll get right to work."

Just over a week later, the *sofer* called us, triumphant. "I've written the *parshiyos* — and they're beautiful," he said.

"Now we need to bring them to the *battim macher*."

Phew. I hadn't needed to get worried after all. (Not that I can help it too much, Mommy said I started worrying when I was a baby and I never stopped. Even when I was a little kid in a stroller, I asked Tatty what would happen if the wheel came off.) I was so excited at the thought of having my tefillin — winding the black straps around my arm, putting them on my head, adjusting them with the help of one of those little round mirrors that people keep in their tefillin bags, kiss them ... Tatty had chosen a top *sofer* from Eretz Yisrael to write them — he wanted my tefillin to be the very best they could be.

One thing you should know about my parents — they're not the organized type. Every time I get nervous about it, they reassure me that somehow, they always manage to get there, even if there's some flurry along the way. With my bar mitzvah, though, I — and they — were determined that it would be different. Thanks to my nudging, we had the invitations ready three months before. And my mother said that in two weeks' time, when the freezer wasn't full, she'd start cooking for the bar mitzvah Shabbos. This would be a Menachem-style bar mitzvah, I thought happily to myself. True, there'd been a bit of a misunderstanding about the tefillin, but it seemed like everything was back on track, once again.

Did I say on track? Well ... Here's what happened.

The *battim macher* took a couple of weeks, and when he finally called to tell us that the tefillin were ready, I was jubilant. There was no time to lose — in a little over two weeks, it would be a month before my bar mitzvah, the day when my father said I would begin putting the tefillin on, like a test run before the real thing.

"And you remembered that my son is left-handed?"

"Left handed?" the *battim macher* groaned. "I'd forgotten."

I still don't really understand the difference between

righties' and lefties' tefillin, but apparently it's quite a job to adjust the straps correctly. And of course, that would take more time. That horrible, niggling worry feeling crept into the pit of my stomach.

"*Nu, nu*. Better get on with it then," my father said, flashing me a half-grin that I couldn't return.

Baruch Hashem, it didn't take too long to adjust the tefillin, and then came phone call after phone call as my father tried to find someone coming from Eretz Yisrael who could bring the tefillin over for me. Eventually, we found someone leaving Eretz Yisrael in two days' time, who would bring the tefillin to Manchester. Then we got hold of my uncle, who's learning in the Mir, asking him to pick up the tefillin from the *battim macher* and deliver them to the family who would be bringing them.

Well, that all went smoothly enough, and I was starting to believe that maybe I would get my tefillin on time, after all. I was very excited — and relieved, too, that I didn't have to borrow a pair of tefillin to use on the very first morning that I was going to perform this special mitzvah.

My tefillin got to Manchester safely, but now we were faced with another question (conundrum, my father called it). How could we get them from Manchester to Gateshead? My mother called all her friends who live in Manchester, and my father asked his *chavrusas*, the men in shul, our neighbors ... but nobody knew of anyone traveling from Manchester to Gateshead within the next few days.

When I saw what was happening, and how every call just wasn't working out, I was so upset that I locked myself in my bedroom. I knew that Mommy and Tatty were working very hard, but it seemed like all their work was coming to nothing. This wouldn't happen in anyone else's home, I thought to myself, as I pulled down the lists I'd made for my bar mitzvah and started looking through them.

Thank you gift for Mommy and Tatty — check.

Hat — check

Shoes — check

Tie — check

Spare batteries for my camera (in case mommy's isn't working) — check

The only thing that wasn't yet organized was the item at the very top of my list. Tefillin.

Today was Monday. Wednesday was the special day that had been circled on the calendar in my sister's silver pen. Wednesday was the day when I was supposed to don my tefillin for the very first time. And it seemed like on Wednesday, my tefillin would be stuck in Manchester — a hundred or so miles away.

Eventually, my stomach starting rumbling, and I had to come out for supper. As I headed down the stairs, I heard my mother answer the phone. She sounded excited. I leaned over the banister to hear what she was saying.

"Oh, that's wonderful! Thanks so much for letting me know."

I heard my mother put the phone down and then she called me. I raced down the rest of the stairs.

"Do you remember hearing about Camp Sunshine?"

I nodded. My friend Chaim's sister goes each year. It's for children with special needs. "Well, the camp ends tomorrow. I'm sure the bus will drop off some of the children in Manchester before coming on to Gateshead. If we can get your tefillin on that bus, you'll have them by Wednesday morning."

Whoopee! I held out my hand for my little brother to give me a high five.

My mother had already dialed the number of the camp.

I had to give it to her. She might not be too organized, but she really gets down to things. And the number of phone calls she'd already made to try and get my tefillin in time ...

"Uh ... Thanks, Mommy," I said.

She smiled at me even as she began talking to the camp director and asking him about the route home.

"I'd love to help you out," the director said, "but there are only a few children here from Manchester, so we're transporting them in a separate van. The main bus is heading straight to Gateshead."

I could see the tears in my mother's eyes as she put down the phone, and I felt so bad for her that I almost stopped feeling sorry for myself.

"You're a good boy, Menachem," she said, as I handed her a cup of cinnamon tea. "And don't worry. *Hakadosh Baruch Hu* will help us get those tefillin here right on time for you."

The next day was Tuesday. My parents were still trying to think of how they could get hold of the tefillin, but inside, I'd kind of given up hope. *So, I'll wear a pair of borrowed tefillin*, I thought to myself, trying hard to make peace with the situation. But it wasn't so easy.

When I got home from school though, I found my mother, once again, with the telephone receiver clapped to her ear. She was on the phone with my uncle in Manchester — the one who had my tefillin.

"Guess what happened?" she said, once she had finished talking. "The bus taking the children home from camp started overheating on the highway, so the driver decided to switch busses. Instead of coming straight to Gateshead, the bus is right now at the depot in ...

"Manchester!" I exclaimed.

"Got it in one. So I called Uncle Duvid."

"But Uncle Duvid doesn't have a car. How's he supposed to get the tefillin over there?"

"So listen to this *hashgachah pratis*. Just today, Uncle

Duvid's father had a hospital appointment, and he asked Uncle Duvid to drive him there. He let him keep the car afterward so he can run a few errands."

Uncle Duvid grabbed my tefillin and zoomed off in his car to the bus depot, where twenty special-needs children were getting off the old, overheating bus and boarding a new one. The helpers were busy transferring all the suitcases from one bus to another, and Uncle Duvid handed out *rugelach* and drinks to all the children to keep them occupied while they were waiting. Then he gave my precious tefillin to the camp director, who, as a special favor, offered to deliver the tefillin directly to our house.

Wednesday morning. I woke up early, washed *negel vasser*, and ran down the stairs, taking the last five in a flying leap. Today was the day! And there, ready in a beautiful blue velvet bag with *Menachem* embroidered in silver, were my brand-new tefillin. They were waiting for me on the dining-room table ... like they'd been sitting there since the day I was born.

Far Away From Home

My name is Feivish and I am an old, old man. Why, you ask, is my tale included in this book, a collection of stories about children? It is because this story took place a long, long time ago, when I, too, was a child. And it's a very special story, one that I think you will always remember.

Where do you come from? America? Israel? South Africa? England? I don't come from any of those places. I come from a country in Europe called Austria. I didn't live there for long, though. When I was 9 years old, my parents put me on a train that carried children out of Europe, far away from the war that was brewing. There were a lot of children on the train and it was given a name: the *Kindertransport.* The *Kindertransport* charged through Europe to a port in the Netherlands, where we boarded a ship to Southampton, England. Unfortunately for me, as I traveled away from danger, I moved far away from my home and my family.

When we arrived in England, we were taken to stay with

different families. Mostly these families were kind and welcoming; sometimes, though, they were harsh and cruel. The story I want to tell you took place while I was staying with the Finnigans, in a tiny village in the middle of the Welsh countryside.

The duffle coat I wore was scratchy. I fingered the wide buttons, easing them through the thin leather loops and twisting them around and around. It was cold, bitter cold, and since I had left my mother and family, the cold had wrapped its icy fingers around my heart, as well.

They were good people, really, Mr. and Mrs. Finnigan. They meant well. But just like they would never understand the world I came from, I would never really understand the world that they were part of.

She was broad-shouldered and double-chinned, waging a war on dust and dirt — and the Germans, of course. He was quieter, and I wasn't really sure what he did. Grew the largest squash in the region, that I did know, and fixed his own tractor. When he was inclined, he fixed the neighbor's tractor, as well. But he didn't want people to know. Scared that they would enlist him as a mechanic, or put him to some other use for the war effort. "And you know," he would say as he puffed on his pipe, "that I make plenty of effort already."

I wanted to tell him that no, it wasn't enough effort. That my family were over in Europe, in danger from the war. But I didn't.

"Cat got your tongue?" he would ask me. Wordlessly, I would shake my head.

I knew what they said in England, I'd learned a lot in the nine months I'd been living here. *Children should be seen and not heard*. Even if I didn't feel like a child.

Was it only nine months before that the train doors had opened and I had stepped out onto the platform of Kings Cross train station? In the confusion that followed, the clatter of porters and trunks and billeting officers screaming out names and numbers in English — a language I didn't yet know — I had somehow been separated from my friends. We'd all been scattered through the country: Dorset, Yorkshire, Wales, to villages and farms. Sent to live with families who had names like Jones and McNerfy and Smith, and we were politely but firmly reminded that just like our voices, our Jewishness could be seen but not heard.

The *Kindertransport*: it saved the lives of thousands of Jewish children. Back home in Austria, they were probably dreaming of our freedom, of our lives and safety. But we dreamed of warmth and hominess, of the sweet sound of our fathers' learning and our rebbis' sharp retorts. We dreamed of our mother's homemade challah and our Bobbe's melt-in-the-mouth sponge cake.

Sally Phillips was the name of the billeting officer for South Wales. She had blond hair and a pointy nose and wore silver-framed glasses. She was in charge of making sure all the children had a family to stay with, and she tried hard. She smoothed it over when the Finnigans complained that I wouldn't eat the roast beef they prepared for Sunday lunch, and she persuaded them to leave me alone on Shabbos, and not to force me to help out round the farm.

She also promised that if I made the effort to settle down, to be good and calm and helpful, then she would try and arrange for me to spend the Jewish holidays at one of the religious communities. That was a bribe if there ever was one.

So I behaved. I learned to milk the cows and groom the horse; I learned how to light a coal fire in the fireplace — big coals at the bottom, smaller ones on top, light some paper and fan the flames until the coals catch. Mr. and Mrs. Finnigan were fair, even if they weren't very warm, and they told Miss Phillips that I was trying my best. So, come Pesach,

Miss Phillips arranged that I could go and stay with a *frum* family living in Manchester for two weeks.

What a joy to be living among *Yidden* again! To have a proper Shabbos table, with challahs and wine; to go to shul for *Kabbalas Shabbos* and hear the Torah reading on Shabbos morning. Shabbos in Wales was a long, lonely day that I spent in my bedroom, davening and reading and dreading the moment when the Finnigans would call me down to help them with anything from threading a needle (Mrs. Finnigan couldn't see too well and this was hard for her) to weeding the garden. Each time I shook my head and tried to keep my voice firm. "Sorry, but it's my holy day today," I would tell them.

Each time I told them that they would nod and give a little frown. "You'd best be off to your bedroom, then," they would say. So that's where I returned.

As I was saying, Pesach in Manchester was a dream. And when I returned home to the Finnigans, I resolved to be on my best behavior. Maybe, just maybe, Sally would send me off to another *frum* family for the *Yamim Nora'im* and Succos. It was that thought — the vision of being in shul on Yom Kippur, staring at the gleaming white *paroches* and hearing the *chazzan* chant *Kol Nidrei* — that got me through the next few months.

To be sure, after Pesach, with the days getting longer and the frosty chill melting into mellow spring days, life was easier. The sun streamed in through the bedroom window early, and I grew to love the smell of the soft earth. And as long as I helped out enough, the Finnigans were friendly.

Sally did her best for me, and come Rosh Hashanah, I was on a train to Sunderland. It was colder in Sunderland than in Wales, and the Northerners' heavy accent made it hard for me to understand what they said. But still, the Kahns were special people, and they did their best to make me feel at home. Their children had all left home years before, and I spent hours poring over a set of encyclopedias: huge books with beautiful pictures.

The Kahns had different *minhagim* than those I was used to. At home, we had a table filled with *simanim*; the Kahns had only apple and honey. The challah was bought in a store and it was chewy. It didn't melt in my mouth like my mother's challah. Somehow, being at the Kahns made my loneliness worse, and when I accompanied Mr. Kahn to shul, I davened to Hashem with all my heart that He keep my family safe. I knew there was a war raging in Europe, and I prayed that my family would escape the fighting and that we would be reunited.

The second day of Rosh Hashanah, Mrs. Kahn was laid up in bed with the flu, and so Mr. Kahn and I ate alone at the Yom Tov table. After that, I didn't see her until I left, when she came down the stairs, coughing and sneezing, to wave me goodbye.

When I asked Sally about Yom Kippur, she gave me a look that said, *Don't push your luck.* "You've had Passover and the New Year," she said. "I can't always manage this, y'know. It takes a lot of arranging and a lot of paperwork. Especially because Mrs. Kahn's feeling poorly and she can't have you back."

I nodded, unable to speak. My shoulders slumped down and tears welled up in my eyes. Sally looked at me for a long moment. "I'll do me best," she said.

I davened hard all that week. I knew that that was the week of *Selichos*, but I didn't have a book of *Selichos* and I didn't know any by heart, so I made up my own:

"Please, Hashem, make Sally find me a *frum* family to stay with for Yom Kippur and Succos. Please Hashem, take care of my family. Please Hashem, make them come and find me."

It was with a smile that Sally told me that she had turned

the earth upside down and found me a place to stay for Yom Kippur. This time, I'd be traveling South, to London. That made me nervous.

"But what about all the bombs dropping over London?" I asked.

"Nah, it's pretty quiet at the moment," Sally said. "Otherwise I wouldn't be allowed to send you there."

So that's how I found myself on the train to London, my best shirt and socks tied up in a brown-paper parcel, a slip of paper in my hand with the address of the Weiners, in Stamford Hill. I found my way there all right, and as soon as I stepped through the door and put my parcel down on the bed they showed me, they began to ply me with food.

"Here," said Mrs. Weiner, offering me a steaming plate of kugel. "Don't forget that it's a fast day tonight."

I made a *berachah* and wolfed down the food and barely had time to wash my hands and face and change into my best shirt before I was called downstairs for the *seudah hamafsekes*.

"Why, you're not much more than skin and bone," said Mrs. Weiner, looking me up and down. "Tuck in, my boy. And I don't think you should be fasting much past breakfast, if you ask me."

I looked at her.

"You're not yet bar mitzvah, are you?"

I shook my head.

"Well, then, there's nothing to talk about. Now eat up and then you'll be hurrying to shul for *Kol Nidrei*."

The shul was cramped and the air was heavy. By craning my neck I could just see the gleam of the white *paroches*. A sudden silence fell, and then a rustling sound as hundreds of fingers flipped through the *machzorim* to find the place. *Kol Nidrei*.

And then, through the silence, I heard a voice that seemed

like it came from the heavens themselves. It was a pure voice, a soulful voice, a voice filled with sobbing and sadness and awe and holiness.

"*Kol Nidrei . . .*"

I gasped.

It was the voice of my Tatty.

"Tatty!" I yelled. "Tatty! Tatty!"

All around me, faces turned to stare, but I didn't care. "Tatty! Tatty!"

I pushed my way to the front of the shul. There, dressed like an angel in his *kittel*, and standing in front of the huge *siddur* of the *shaliach tzibbur*, was my father.

He looked up and saw me and held out his arms. I fell into his embrace.

That Yom Kippur, the day all children return to their Tatty in *Shamayim*, Hashem returned me to my Tatty on earth.

On the Fast Track

Take a look at me. A good stare. That's right. Y'see anything wrong? No. I look like you, act like you, talk like you ... I go to school and I come home and I have to put up with my annoying brothers and I like to bake cookies and I hate doing the dishes. There is something different, though.

I have Cystic Fibrosis.

For those of you who don't know, Cystic Fibrosis is a genetic condition that affects the lungs, causing them to give off extra mucus. Doesn't sound like a big deal, and in my case, *baruch Hashem*, it isn't such a big deal. I have just a mild case, but there are some people who struggle with every breath and who are constantly fighting very serious infections. These infections can actually be life threatening. I don't like to think about this too much, but I want to tell you so that you know how thankful I am that Hashem's made me pretty healthy.

One of the ways in which I do feel my illness (besides the

constant rounds at the doctors and my twice-weekly physical therapy sessions) is in my sinuses. The mucus builds up and every year or so, I need to undergo surgery to clean them out.

So that's how it happened that I was there at the hospital, and the doctor had just given me the pronouncement: surgery time. Now, that made me feel very yucky inside. I get very nervous before the operation, and afterward I always feel nauseous and weak. But, I also knew that hospitals take their time over these things, so it would be at least a few months until the surgery was scheduled.

"There is a slight problem, this time around," Dr. Lacy told me, looking over his glasses. "Professor White is moving out of town. I have no idea who his replacement will be."

My mother nodded and didn't say anything, but it was clear she wasn't happy. Professor White has been my surgeon since I could remember. He's an expert, with years of experience treating kids with CF. To hear that he was no longer in the picture made the surgery much more scary.

Dr. Lacy, though, remained cheerful. "You know the way things are here in these South African hospitals," he said, shaking his head. "By the time you get the ultrasound done, the new surgeon will undoubtedly be a dab hand."

And with that, he opened his door and, with a polite little bow, showed us out.

The next stop on our agenda was the ultrasound unit, to make an appointment. I'm always tired when we're done with Dr. Lacy, what with the journey to the hospital and all, and every time I ask Mommy if we can just go straight home. (That's another way in which I feel my CF: I get more tired than other people.) My mother won't budge, though. She says that when you take the trouble to make the appointment in person, you get seen sooner. I really don't know whether she's right or wrong, but I know when it's worth arguing. And in this, Mommy never gives in.

When we got there, the receptionist at the desk was looking at her nail polish: it was dark blue with silver stars. She didn't look too busy, but then again, for some reason, the waiting time for an ultrasound was always at least three months.

My mother cleared her throat. "A-hem."

The receptionist looked up, and after blowing on her nails (I suppose she was worried that they were getting dusty), she took the letter and forms that my mother handed over. She looked them over and disappeared into one of the back rooms.

A minute later, a technician walked out, holding our forms. "Are you — ah — Rai . . . Raizel Ka . . . Katzberg?"

They always had a hard time with my name. I nodded.

"Well, come along then."

"What?" my mother interrupted.

"Well, no one turned up for the appointment, so I can do the ultrasound right now."

Wow! This was something that had never happened before. I could see my mother's mind working, saying: *See, I told you it's worth making the appointment in person.*

The technician did the ultrasound, and soon we were once again walking through the endless hospital hallways.

"I'm just going to stop in at Dr. Lacy and tell him what happened. He might want to take a look at the results."

I groaned. I was hungry and tired. "Do we really have to?"

"Absolutely," said my mother, striding toward the bank of elevators.

Back we went to Dr. Lacy's lilac waiting room. We'd been there for less than 2 minutes when he appeared, ushering a patient out of his consulting rooms. For the first time ever, I appreciated the fact that he's such a gentleman: it meant that he caught sight of us and then asked us what was up.

My mother jumped up and told him about the ultrasound.

"Well, well, well," he said. He apologized to his next patient and took us into his consulting rooms, where he examined the results of the ultrasound.

"Truly unprecedented," he kept muttering to himself. He'd never, ever heard of anyone receiving an ultrasound in less than two months — let alone on the spot. He lifted up the phone and dialed Professor White's number.

Surprisingly enough, Professor White answered the phone. When he heard about the ultrasound, he gave his usual chuckle and asked if he should follow the technician's example.

"What does he mean?" I asked.

"It means, young lady," said Dr. Lacy, "that he's prepared to operate on you this very afternoon."

I took a deep breath and I could feel my hands start to tremble. My mother whipped out her cell phone and started punching in Tatty's number.

Two minutes later, Dr. Lacy's phone rang again. It was Professor White, informing him that he'd found an anesthetist. Had I eaten in the last six hours, he wanted to know.

"Well, I had breakfast this morning," I said, thinking of the soggy cornflakes I'd forced myself to swallow before we left the house.

My mother looked at her watch. "That was probably about . . . five and a half hours ago."

"Wonderful." Even from our places on the other side of the desk, we heard Professor White booming down the phone. "Tell them to come right over."

My mother called my father at work, and he rushed home to pick up my pajamas, a robe, and my favorite book, driving straight on to the hospital. Then she arranged with a friend to do carpool instead of her.

That very afternoon, I had the surgery — the very last operation that Professor White performed before he headed out of the state and set up a practice 700 miles away.

Leib

He's Up Here, Too

Winter's finally over and boy, am I glad. I was just about done with all those long, dark, cold afternoons where the only thing to do was to swipe that Monopoly credit card over and over and over, just for the fun of it, and read the same old comic books for the billionth time. Now it's light for longer and Mommy lets me ride my bike and play outside when I come home from school.

Last spring, me and my friend Zalmy made a clubhouse out in his garden. Zalmy's house is at the edge of town, and his garden ... well, you could make believe that that's part of the countryside, too. It goes on and on almost forever and there's a cute little fish pond at one side that one time we tried to shunt into a canal, and huge bushes that we trimmed down from the inside to make a good hiding place. Toward the back there are rabbit burrows, and sometimes we see rabbits run out, heading to the rows of carrots and cabbages and squash that Zalmy's mother always plants in the winter. Each spring she wonders why they don't grow too well.

We built the clubhouse against the back fence; we had to be careful about the nails — my mother wasn't too thrilled about the number of times I came home with ripped pants, but she was pretty happy that I was so busy. She's good friends with Zalmy's mother, and more than once I heard them on the phone, talking about how all the hammering and sawing was improving our fine motor skills and stick-to-itiveness and how it was a good outlet for us. Whatever.

This spring, though, we figure we're going to try something more ambitious. Y'see, one of the great things about Zalmy's garden is the trees. They must be fifty years old, those trees. There's a horse chestnut, and an apple tree that has a great smell, kind of like the apple cobbler my mother makes for Shabbos. And there's a great tall pine tree that's green all year round, and when you stick those pine needles down someone's back, boy, do they get mad ...

My father owns a bakery right next to our shul, and he always says, "Location, location, location." So, for once, I'm going to take his words to heart, as he always asks me to. We're going to build a brand new clubhouse, but this time, it's going to be different. Location, y'see. It's going to be up a tree.

A clubhouse high up in a tree is more of a challenge than a clubhouse on the ground. For starters, we have to build a little platform to keep our tools — hammer, nails, wrench, screwdriver ... You get the idea. Then we have to scavenge for wood, saw it down to just the right length and width; and then we have to get it up that tree.

"How're we going to get all this stuff up there?" I ask Zalmy, pointing to the pile of lumber that we've already collected. Zalmy stares and thinks and walks around and around that tree till I get dizzy watching him.

"Quit the *hakafos*, won't you?"

"Okay, okay. I'm just trying to figure out . . . "

Suddenly, he shoots a high five into the air. "Got it!"

"What?"

"Just watch."

So I watch while Zalmy goes searching through the shed and comes out with his mother's old washing line and half an old bike.

I have to hand it to Zalmy: he's a genius at this stuff. I stand there watching as he's taking the tire off the bike, revealing a metal circle that has a groove just right for a piece of rope — or his mother's old washing line. He climbs up the tree, and I hand him the bike and the washing line, which he ties tightly into place. Then he tells me to tie some of the wood to the end of the washing line, and he starts pedaling with his hands. Round and round, till the rope gets pulled up and with it the wood. See, I told you he's a genius.

The next day, and the next, and the next, we're real busy. I run home from school, dump my bag, grab a cup of juice, and shout goodbye to Mommy. And she tousles my hair (which I hate but she does it anyway), and hands me a bag of supplies — oatmeal cookies, juicy oranges, brownies . . . something to keep us going. And then I hop on my bike, ride three blocks to Zalmy's house, let myself in through the side entrance that leads straight to their garden, stop under the great tall pine tree. I dismount and, leaning my bike against the tree trunk, I climb up on the seat of my bike and grab the lowest branches. Then I hoist myself up. My bike stays there, at the bottom of the tree, so that when I need to come down I can dangle from the lowest branch and, steadying myself on the tree trunk, rest my legs on the seat of my bike and then scramble safely down to the ground.

Between you and me, I would have been happy to build the clubhouse on one of the lower branches. "What?" Zalmy said when I suggested it, "what's the point of that? There won't be any privacy and we won't be able to look down on anyone, either. Besides, Shuky will be able to get in if we make it lower."

I couldn't argue. Shuky is a cute 7-year-old, but he's 7, not 11, and a 7-year-old does not belong in an 11-year-old's clubhouse. Apart from on special occasions, of course, when we'd send him an invitation.

So, we're building that clubhouse high in the tree: when Zalmy's father saw it he shook his head and said that it must be 25 feet high. That's maybe five times the height of a small person (like me).

Today, as usual, I'm racing along the three blocks to Zalmy's house, two thick wedges of apple pie left over from Shabbos bulging out of my pocket. Suddenly, I have this thought. It's more of a Zalmy kind of thought than a Leib kind of thought, but there it is, flashing URGENT at me. *Take a challenge*, it's telling me.

What kind of a challenge? I wonder.

Leave the bike by the house. Then see if you can get up and down the tree without stepping up on the seat.

Nah, I think. After all, we have too much to do today. We're trying to secure the side panels so that we have a sturdy wall.

Do it, whispers the voice. *Just do it.*

I get to Zalmy's house, and, I don't know why, but instead of leaning my bike against the pine tree, I park it against the wall of the house and jog down to the garden. The lowest branch is out of reach, so I wrap my arms around the trunk and try to shimmy up. It's slow going, but I get there eventually, reaching up to the lowest branch and then using the branches like a ladder to climb up. I go higher and higher until I reach the clubhouse. And all the time I'm climbing, I'm wondering to myself, *what did I do that for?*

Zalmy's already up there, and we tuck into the pie before

I get down to some serious work. To secure the side wall, you really have to nail it from the outside. Problem is, those branches aren't strong enough to hold you. Nailing from the inside just doesn't do the job. So then Zalmy figures that we could perch on the branch above, which is strong enough, and lean down to nail the walls. I'm holding the walls in place and Zalmy's hammering and I think it's coming along fine, when I realize that it's pretty late. Mommy would for sure want me home by now. So I say goodbye, step out of the almost-finished clubhouse onto a branch, and all of a sudden, I feel my heart and my mouth and my eyes and my head mush into some kind of kaleidoscope and I'm not sure what I'm feeling first. All I knew is that, at 25 feet above the ground, I've lost my footing. Whoooooaaa! I'm hurtling down, down, down to the ground.

When I open my eyes again, I see my mother's face peering over me. I feel woozy and strange and I suddenly realize that my whole body is shooting with pain. I hear a paramedic put his mouth to his walkie talkie and say, "Casualty has regained consciousness, over."

I close my eyes again and feel myself being wheeled into an ambulance, and then into the hospital. They give me a shot and then all goes hazy and dark.

When I wake up, I'm lying in a ward, Mommy and Tatty next to me.

"What . . . what's going on?"

"You're being kept in for observation," Tatty explains. "Do you remember what happened?"

I do kind of remember, but thinking hurts me so I let Tatty explain. "You fell from the tree in Zalmy's garden. You've fractured two ribs and you've received eleven stitches on your head."

My hand creeps up to my head and touches the soft bandage.

"Awake then now, are you?" A nurse comes along, takes

a look at some papers clipped to the end of my bed and then starts rolling up my sleeve and strapping something around it with Velcro.

"Just taking your blood pressure. Just to be safe."

The band swells and then lets out the air and beeps.

"Excellent," says the nurse, as she notes down the numbers. "You'll be right as rain in a few days. At least it was a clean fall."

Mommy shakes her head. "What do you mean?"

"I mean, your son is very lucky there was nothing sitting there at the bottom of the tree: a table or a chair ..."

"Or a bike?"

My mother shudders. The nurse nods. "Or a bike. His injuries would have been much, much more serious if he'd fallen onto the metal frame of a bike."

I lie back on the hospital bed. I'm feeling drowsy again and a little confused as well. There's a little thought though, niggling at me, kind of like the way when you have a loose tooth and your tongue keeps creeping back to that spot in your mouth. So what is this thought? What is it?

"Oh!" I exclaim.

"What?"

I shake my head. I don't want to tell my mother, at least not yet. She'll get too freaked out. But I realize that there was a reason I parked my bike by the house and not under the tree, like I do every single day. Whether down on the ground or 25 feet up a tree, Hashem's taking good care of me.

Libby

Just Another Boring Bus Ride

I still don't know why I did it. But that Sunday morning, when my little sis (not really so little, she is 13, after all) was packing up her bathing suit, consulting her lists, and making phone calls, I volunteered to come along and help her out.

There's always been something inside me that's a bit ... well ... jealous of the way Freidy organizes her swimming group. She coordinates between the pool, the lifeguard, and the six kids she's coaxing to give up doggy paddle and try breast stroke. Teaching the kids to splash through their boundaries, is how my father puts it.

Freidy was busy stuffing another one of her lists (I never even write lists, let alone follow them) into her knapsack and hunting around for her bathing cap and I suddenly thought that it might be fun to join her.

"Join me? As in, swim?" Freidy said.

"Not swim." Unlike Freidy, I never go near the water unless . . . I'm pushed in (which has happened before). "I'll just come with you on the bus."

"Wow, what an exciting morning you're going to have. A 15-minute ride on a London bus."

I ignored the sarcasm. "Okay, then. So I'm coming for the company."

"For company," Freidy repeated, looking at me as if I had lost my mind.

I did wonder that myself, actually. Traveling on London busses isn't my first choice of a fun Sunday morning trip. For some reason, though, I really felt like going this time.

Better than the history report I was due to give in, anyway.

I was ready in under 6 minutes, and I joined Freidy at the front door as she tucked a bulging wallet into her coat pocket. "It's the first Sunday of the month," she said by way of explanation.

"Don't get it."

"On the first Sunday of each month we have to pay for the whole month of swimming. The parents give me the money and I organize it all."

Typical.

We walked down the street together to the bus stop, where Freidy's swim group meets us.

One, two, three, four, five, six ponytailed heads climbed up onto the bus and showed their bus passes. Freidy and I followed.

It's a 15-minute ride to the pool, and I was glad that we'd be getting off so fast. The bus was crowded — every seat was taken and there must have been at least ten people standing in the aisles, trying to keep upright as the bus lurched around corners and braked at traffic lights. We were all jammed together, and I kept my chin pointed slightly toward the ceiling, just to have some air to breathe. Meanwhile, Freidy had spotted one of her teachers, so she was trying to act all grown-up and responsible. Not that she had to act, you understand, because for Freidy it just comes naturally. But I think she wanted to make double sure that the teacher would get the right impression.

So that's how she didn't notice the skinny boy with a pale face and greasy hair sidle toward her. He had a whole row of earrings: starting down at the earlobe and going up to the top of his ear.

I watched as a hand reached out and gently, gently began unzipping the side pocket of Freidy's coat. The pocket that bulged. The one that held the wallet that held all the money.

With a flash, I realized that there might have been a very good reason why I had decided to go along for the ride that morning. I grabbed Freidy's coat, and, in doing so, yanked the thief's hand away from the pocket — and the wallet. "Thief! Thief!" I called and everyone started shouting and moving and the bus driver was yelling, "What's going on back there?" The boy fell backward, and then, as the bus pulled in at the next stop, he jumped to his feet and ran out of the bus onto the street, not once looking back.

"You okay?" I asked Freidy. She was shaking and her swimming girls were giggling nervously.

She nodded.

We got off just a couple of stops later, and I walked them all the way to the pool. By now I wasn't worried for them: with every step, Freidy was regaining her composure.

"See," I told her as I waved goodbye. "Who said that a ride on a London bus is really such a boring Sunday morning trip?"

And Freidy had to agree.

Rabbis and Renters

What's it like being the rabbi's son? I guess that depends on what kind of rabbi. In our community, it's ... well ... uh, I guess you could say it keeps me on my toes. For one thing, I can never slip out of shul during the *haftarah*. If I do, the three old men who sit behind me won't know when to stand up or sit down.

There's old Mr. Cohen, who always starts singing *Adon Olam* first — even before the *chazzan* — and always in the same boring tune. There's Mr. Schumacher, who pours the Kiddush wine into my father's *becher*, and stands tapping his feet until my father makes Kiddush. I think it's because he can't wait to get a bite of my mother's schmaltz herring. Then there's Mr. Lederman, who talks all through the Kiddush about his stocks and shares. All types and stripes, as Abba says with a smile.

The shul started off in our dining room. That was hard, especially when I was younger, because we had to keep quiet the whole way through the davening, and on Shabbos morning, that's long — especially with my father's *derashah*. I did also feel kind of cool — especially when our cousins would come stay and we would stand at the door of my father's study and peep at the *aron kodesh* that was kept there.

Then the shul moved to an apartment of its own: whoa, our very own premises. Abba was sooo excited about that, and Ima was happy to have the dining room back and not have to stack up fifty chairs before each Shabbos meal. Recently, though, even the apartment has gotten too small.

You see, a couple years ago, a high-tech park opened up near our neighborhood, and lots of younger families moved in to be near where they work. They all found our shul and my father (or he found them), and now most of them come every Shabbos. "We've got to keep on our toes," Abba told Ima, and he set to work organizing bagel breakfasts and sizzling summer barbecues — all with some *divrei Torah*, of course, to teach the families about Shabbos and keeping kosher and how to be a proud Jew.

"It's not enough," my mother always said after these events, when she sat back on the couch after all her hard work of shopping and preparing and socializing and cleaning up. "An adult hears a few ideas, maybe likes them, maybe not. It takes a lot of time and energy until they might begin to absorb and change. If we get their kids, though, while they're still little, and teach them about Yom Tov and *middos* and about the *heilige* Torah . . ."

I have to hand it to my mother. When she thinks something needs to be done, she goes right ahead (maybe that's one of the reasons why we ended up living in a place where's there's not even a kosher pizza store). So she approached Colette and Yvonne and Kay and all the other young mothers and asked them to enroll their children in the new shul kindergarten.

“A kindergarten? But where will it be?”

“Who will run it?”

“What’s on the syllabus?”

“What’s the mission statement?”

The questions came flying at Ima, but she didn’t mind.

“I’ll run it right here in our home — what better atmosphere could you want? It’ll be like a second home. You want to know about a mission statement? Well, obviously to learn about shapes and colors and seasons. There’ll be painting and dance and music and outside play. And the children will learn all about the Jewish holidays and the mitzvot.”

“Mitz-what?” asked Joanne.

“Mitzvot,” Ima explained. “Commandments. Like, good deeds.”

“Oh. Well, that certainly sounds nice, rebbetzin, but it’s not practical. Our older son Joey needs to be dropped off at the other side of town, so we send Kathy to the kindergarten next door.”

Ima’s face fell. That kindergarten wasn’t Jewish. Kathy would spend the year drawing pumpkins for Halloween and learning to sing their holiday songs. Ima said goodbye to Joanne and hurried back into the house, shaking her head and mumbling to herself. It was the same with everyone she asked. All the mothers liked the idea. They looked up to Ima, thinking that she’s calm and kind and a great mother. They would all just love to send their teeny tots to the rebbetzin, they said. But it just wasn’t practical. The elementary school was on the other side of town “and you just know what the morning traffic’s like,” they told her, one after the other. For now, Ima had to forget her plans, and all her dreams of cute little 3-year-olds constructing miniature succahs from Play-Doh and wooden lollypop sticks.

"*Baruch Hashem, baruch Hashem*, every rabbi should have this problem," Abba said each Shabbos as he squeezed his way down the aisle of the overcrowded shul. But every week, over the *cholent*, he said the same thing: "We have to find a solution. We can't go on like this for much longer." My father spent a lot of time talking to different organizations and trying to get money from different places, but it was too difficult. In the end, he shelved the idea of building his own shul and decided to rent a house nearby.

"But it's so expensive, way beyond our means," Ima protested. "And that's not even including all the renovations."

"True, true," Abba said, stroking his beard. "But *Hakadosh Baruch Hu* will help. Besides, I've got the whisper of a plan in my head."

A few weeks later, my father had a meeting with a lawyer and the owner and he signed loads and loads of papers. Then and planners and builders and renovators came and took over the place: a large house on the other side of our street.

The fun had begun. After school each day, we stood, watching all the builders with their yellow helmets, pencils behind their ears and tape measures hanging from their pockets. Trucks drove up, all the time, filled with tiles and pipes, kitchen stuff, and sinks for the bathroom. Every day or two, Abba would let us come with him on a grand inspection. Sometimes we even took photos so we'd remember what the place looked like when it was a building site.

While all this was happening, my father was talking to all the connections he knew about the house. "We're using the basement and the first floor. There's the second floor completely available. If I find someone to rent it from me, then we'll be able to afford the rent."

"And if you don't?" I asked.

"There goes Mr. Worrier again," Abba said. "*Hakadosh Baruch Hu* will help. He always does."

I nodded and, that afternoon, I davened Minchah with as much *kavannah* as I could, asking Hashem to help us find a tenant for the second floor of the shul.

That night, Abba came back home and, instead of throwing his jacket on the couch he grabbed the baby and danced with her around the living room.

"We've got renters!" he sang, and then he continued:

"We couldn't ask for more
'Cause they want the second floor;
For painting, *parshah*, play
And they even want to pay!"

Abba explained that the preschool class that was part of the local day school was overfull, and the school governors decided that it's crazy that so many parents are schlepping across town to drop off their children. So they decided to open up a new preschool class . . . right across the street, on the second floor of Abba's shul.

But what I didn't realize straight away was that if parents are dropping off one child at a preschool, they want to have their other kids nearby. That week, the phone didn't stop ringing. "It's Colette. Are you still interested in running a playgroup for next year?"

"Of course," my mother said happily.

"Then please put my Jordan down on your list."

By Shabbos, my mother had eight kids — just the number she wanted to open up her playgroup. My father had a tenant for the shul. And all of us had one big celebration — for us, for the shul, and for all the little Jewish children who would be learning about shofars and Shabbos and what it means to be a Jew.

Oooooouch!

"Whoopee!"

All five of us let out loud cheers when the announcement was made. Tatty sat there, at the head of the Shabbos table, hiding a smile, and shaking his head in mock weariness.

It was all arranged. Instead of summer camps and day camps, we'd be heading off to JFK airport to vacation in … Eretz Yisrael! For three whole weeks we'd be licking melting ice creams and getting jolted on those funny long busses, and going to the pool with my cousins, and tiptoeing around my grandmother's apartment with all those china models that could smash … what could be better?!

After we got the news I phoned my cousins every week, and they told us loads of fun stuff to do — trips and places to go and things. I wrote it all down and, two weeks before we were supposed to leave, I mapped out a schedule, a whole list of what we could do — when, and where. Mommy was real impressed when she saw how I'd drawn it out neatly, dividing the days with a ruler, and color coding the different areas and what trips would be good for which age group. "I should have let you organize the tickets, as well," she told me and twirled my *peyos* behind my ears — I hate it when she does that. "I'm going to talk about all your ideas with Tatty," she said, "and I'm sure that even if we don't stick to your ... ahem ... itinerary all the time, it will help make this trip one to remember."

I was a little disappointed, but I understood. After all, there was other stuff to schedule in, like shopping for food and making Shabbos. But it's Mommy's job to worry about those things, not mine.

With all the shopping and packing and organizing left to be done, the weeks flew by so fast. Before I even had time to complain that I couldn't wait, there were six bulging suitcases sitting in the front hallway of the house, waiting for the van that would pick us up at 4 in the morning.

One of my cousins, who's also called Naftali, had suggested that we spend a few days up north: visiting *kevarim*, touring Tzfat, hiking to the Banyas, and kayaking down the River Dan. I thought it was a fantastic idea, and I included it in my schedule, for the middle week of our trip. I colored those days in light blue, to remind us of all the great water sports there are up in the Golan and the Galil. I pointed it out to Mommy and Tatty, and I told them that even if they didn't want to do the rest of the stuff I had planned, this one was sooo amazing it would be just terrible to skip it.

It turned out that we really did do most of the things that I'd planned — even if not on the same day and time that I'd scheduled. And even though Mommy nixed the three-day desert experience where we'd sleep overnight in Bedouin tents, she and Tatty thought that spending a few days up north would be a great idea (too bad there aren't so many *kevarim* down south. . . . maybe that would have convinced her. . . .).

So there we were, standing in line to get our kayaks. It was hot, boiling in fact, so hot that the air above the river shimmered. I felt like just jumping into that river with a huge splash. It seemed like a lot of other people also thought that it would be a great kayak day, as the line was long, and it kept on growing.

We were all standing there, wondering whether Mommy and Tatty would buy us more ice-pops, sipping water, fanning ourselves with our caps and sunhats, and waiting for the van full of empty kayaks to pull up so that our turn would finally come.

I look up to see Mommy deep in conversation. "Hey, Naftali, say hi to Mrs. Lichtig." I nodded my head. "Hi," I said.

"Guess what? Mrs. Lichtig's sister is Mrs. Freidman from next door."

"Oh."

"Oh."

"And her sister-in-law sat next to me in seminary."

It sounded like they were having a real schmooze and a half, so I gave another polite smile and left them to it.

It didn't take too much longer before we were scrambling into the overblown, leaky rubber dinghys. Me and Chani and Chaim were in one, and Mommy and Tatty and little Moishy were in another. My feet got soaked right away — the bottom of the kayak filled with water as soon as we moved out into the river. I didn't mind. I was thinking about plopping down on the bottom of the boat so that all of me would get wet. Delish.

We traveled downstream, pushed along by the current, and paddling with a set of large wooden oars. We could have managed without the oars, really; we weren't too good at coordinating, and instead of moving forward, we ended up rowing around and around in circles.

"Here, give me the oar!" I told Chaim.

"No! Why should I?"

" 'Cause this is useless. We're not going anywhere."

He shrugged.

"C'mon, we'll switch off afterward."

He shook his head.

We tried rowing together again, but it was useless. I leaned over to grab the oar, but Chaim snatched it away. It was just at that moment that Chani leaned forward. The oar went flying into her face, hitting her right by her eye with a smack!

"Aaaaah!" she yelled. She clutched her cheek and began sobbing. Chaim and I looked at each other. We both felt bad, but I knew that it was really my fault. Pits. I should have been more grown up, I knew I should. And now I'd ruined a real fun trip and I'd get into trouble and ... and Chani was *still* crying. Was that just because she's a girl or was she really hurt?

"Let me see," I said, and I jerked her arm away from her face. I was a little rough, but that's what happens when you feel bad.

"Oh, my," I said.

In the place where she'd been hit was a large, red mark. Her face was getting more and more swollen, like a bicycle pump was blowing air into it, and it didn't look pretty.

"What should we do?" I wailed. Mommy and Daddy were pretty far in front, and I had no idea what I should do to stop Chani's face swelling so badly. Now it was turning all crazy colors, too.

"Mommy usually puts frozen peas on a place where we get hurt," said Chaim.

"Who has frozen peas in the middle of a kayaking trip?" I said, impatiently.

"Well, what about an ice bottle?"

"You're a genius," I yelled and I rummaged through the bags to find the bottles of ice water we'd brought along.

But when I took them out, the ice was melted and the bottles were full of warm water.

"Now what?"

I looked around, desperately, to see if I could see Mommy and Daddy. I thought I heard their voices, but I saw no one.

Then I heard a splash, and a kayak floated alongside. "Everything okay?" a voice asked.

I looked up. It was Mrs. Lichtig, the woman whose sister was our neighbor and whose sister-in-law had sat next to Mommy in seminary.

I could see that she recognized me, too. "You're Naftali, right?" she said.

I nodded. "Er, my sister, Chani, an oar ... Uh, she got hurt."

Mr. Lichtig grabbed the side of our kayak so that his wife could have a proper look at Chani's face. "I've got just the thing," she said, producing a bottle of solid ice.

She handed it to Chani. "It's going to feel cold but you keep it on your face and the swelling will go down in no time," she said. Chani did as she was told, and, sure enough, the swelling started to go down.

"Thank you! Thanks so, so much!" I called to the Lichtigs as they floated down the river. They were there, just at the right time, with just what we needed. And that was something I could never have planned.

Ruti

Especially for Me

I looked at the heap of clothing on my bed and shivered. It happens each year, but it's still a surprise. One day it's summer. The sky is blue without a cloud and the temperatures soar. The very next day (almost), it's rainy and cold. We dig deep in the closets for umbrellas and shake out the coats, wondering if there's anything fun left in the pockets since last year — a coin or a single, lost earring.

So, there I was on Erev Shabbos, shivering in my robe and toweling dry my hair, and wondering what I could wear. I looked at the brown sweater and matching plaid skirt from last year. I had never liked it: you had to be sure to wear thick tights because the skirt was itchy. Anyway it was too small now. So was the burgundy dress. I looked at my usual set of Shabbos clothing: thin cotton dresses and light, puffy skirts that I wore with a Shabbos'dik top. I'd freeze. I shivered just thinking about it.

The rain beat down on the skylight, making such a racket

that my mother didn't hear me when I called. "Mommy! What should I wear?"

As soon as she was sitting down on my bed, looking through my clothes, I knew I'd made a mistake. My mother's eyebrows were all creased and I could see that she was worried. Where did the worry come from? I'll tell you.

My Tatty has an interesting kind of job. He works in a company that makes medicines for people who are sick. But not just sick like a cold or the flu. Really sick. He explained once that making medicines is not like following a recipe for chocolate chip cookies. It's like figuring out that there's such a thing as a cookie to begin with. Imagining that there could be something sweet and filling and a bit chocolaty and really yummy — and making it and then calling it a cookie. Do you get what I mean? In a way, his job is doing the same thing as the first person who ever made a chocolate chip cookie. He doesn't just say, hey, let's make some aspirin because that will take away people's pain. He looks at someone in pain and says, hey, now if we could block those pain messages, maybe that will take away the pain.

But because medicines are for illness, and sometimes the illness starts in just a few tiny cells in a person's body, his job is much, much harder. He has to think and learn and experiment and test out these medicines, to see how they work and to check that they're not dangerous. So that's what my Tatty does — besides all the regular things like learning and davening and helping other people and teaching my little brothers how to ride their bikes.

But my mother was worried because the place where my father works ran out of money. *Funding* they call it. So now Tatty doesn't have a job. And because he doesn't have a job, there's not a lot of spare cash, as Mommy says. Not having spare cash means that there's enough for challah and chicken and milk and yogurt, but not for any extras. I keep wondering what Mommy means by extras. Is a new Shabbos dress an extra?

By the look on Mommy's face, it seems like it is, although she doesn't want it to be.

Inside, I felt a little bit strange: a bit sad and a bit worried mixed up together, and I felt bad that I told Mommy anything at all (although, she would for sure have noticed that I need something new).

"We'll just have to get you something new," she said, as she fingered the plaid skirt I wore last winter.

That Shabbos I wore last year's outfit. I didn't complain once: not about the itchy skirt and not that when I lifted my arms, I was nervous I was going to rip a hole right under the arms. I didn't mention it on Sunday or Monday, but on Tuesday, my mother said that perhaps we'd go shopping the next day. "Great," I said, flashing a grin. Maybe there was spare cash, after all.

On my way to school the next morning, I noticed a large, pink sign on the notice board as you come out of the building: HUGE BLOWOUT SALE! I read the sign carefully and I saw that one of our neighbors was hosting a clothing sale, that very afternoon.

My mother read the same notice and that afternoon we headed to the neighbor's apartment to see if there was anything there that would be good for me.

Compared to my friends, I'm not so fussy about clothing. But it has to suit me and it has to be comfortable and it has to look right. And of course, I wouldn't want to wear a style that no one's wearing any more. I wouldn't either want to wear any styles that no one is wearing yet. Just something normal.

I looked through the racks of clothing and tried on skirts and jumpers and sweater sets and dresses ... but there was nothing that was just what I was looking for.

"What kind of thing do you want?" my neighbor asked.

"Just something . . . normal."

She looked at me for a few moments, and then she disappeared into one of her bedrooms. She came out with a beautiful turquoise and white jumper, made of a fine knit. I tried it on. It was warm but comfortable and it fitted perfectly. The price tag was hanging off of it, and when I took a look, my heart sank. This was one very expensive piece.

I walked out of the changing area and my mother and my neighbor both nodded their heads and grinned. "Perfect. Just right with your coloring."

Another woman was browsing and she stopped and added her two cents worth. "My, it looks like it was made for you."

My neighbor cocked her head to one side and stared. "A little plain around the neckline, perhaps, but nothing that a nice necklace couldn't fix."

Now I was smiling too. But there was the question of the price tag.

"How much?" my mother asked.

"Well," said my neighbor, thinking for a few minutes. "This isn't really in the sale. My mother-in-law sent it for my daughter, but it's too small. I was wondering what to do with it."

My mother caught sight of the price tag. "This is a beautiful outfit. It cost over a hundred dollars."

My neighbor waved her hand. "True, but my mother-in-law bought it on sale. I'll tell you what, just give me $5 for it and we'll call it quits."

"Are you sure?" my mother asked as she reached for her purse.

"Yeah, it's been sitting around since last winter. I'm glad someone will enjoy it."

I walked home, clutching my bag tight. The outfit truly was perfect; the unusual color matched my eyes, and when I'd tried it on, I felt like a princess. I couldn't wait for Shabbos.

At 7:20 a.m. there was a knock on my bedroom door. *At least I organized my schoolbag last night,* I thought as I snuggled deeper under my covers. I could stay in bed for another 10 minutes before I got up for school.

I heard the handle turn and my mother come inside.

"C'mon, Ruti, good morning!" she said, perching at the end of my bed.

"Morning," I mumbled into my pillow.

"I've got something for you as soon as you've washed *negel vasser.*"

How do mothers always know how to do it? I sat up, splashed the cold water over my hands, said *Modeh Ani*, and opened my eyes properly. In my mother's hands was a small, padded envelope. It had my name on it. I looked closer. It was my grandmother's writing.

"From Bubby?"

My mother shrugged. "Looks like it."

I opened the envelope. Inside was a small box covered in white leather. In the box was a necklace: delicate silver beads sprinkled here and there with exquisite turquoise crystals. It was breathtaking.

I held it up. "Stunning," my mother pronounced. A small card fell out.

Darling Ruti,
Saw this necklace and I knew it was made for you.
Enjoy wearing it.
Love, Bubby

That Erev Shabbos, I showered early. I carefully pulled the tags off my new outfit and put it on. I stood in front of the mirror and excitedly fastened my new necklace. The colors matched perfectly. But even before I put it on, I knew that it would. After all, the dress, and the necklace, too, were made especially for me.

Chaya

A Secret and a Siddur

I'm writing the note in my best handwriting, on my Hello Kitty notepaper.

URGENT AND PRIVATE

I print at the top.

MEETING TONIGHT, STRAIGHT AFTER SUPPER, IN MY BEDROOM. C U THERE.

All during supper I tap my feet on the floor and jiggle my legs. Mommy keeps looking at me strangely, and she even asks me what's wrong. "Nothing," I say.

I've never organized a secret meeting before. I've never even been to one.

Supper over, everyone comes running upstairs to my bedroom. They knock once, like I tell them, and then come inside and get cozy on my beanbag, bed, and rug. I sit on the chair, with a pencil and notepad in my hand.

On the top of the page, I print:

MOMMY'S BIRTHDAY

"Okay," I say, once everyone's quiet. "Mommy's birthday is in just one week. What are we going to do for her?"

"Popcorn — you know, the honey flavored one! Bissli! Corn chips! And a humongous birthday cake — "

I shake my head. "Pinny, all you ever think of is your stomach. C'mon, we're trying to think of Mommy now. What would *Mommy* want for her birthday? And don't say 'nash' because we know she hardly eats that stuff." I wave my pencil in the air as I talk so that they see that I'm serious.

Pinny is lying on his stomach, resting his chin on his fist, thinking. I hope he comes up with something good.

"Chaya," he says, "what about a new broom?"

I look at him and shake my head. "Uh, uh. A broom isn't something fun. Something nice. Something that will make Mommy happy and excited."

"Happy and excited," Pinny repeats after me. "Happy and excited."

I think about it too. What would make Mommy happy and excited? Maybe a bunch of flowers, like Tatty buys for Shabbos. That always makes Mommy happy.

Nah, I think to myself. By Wednesday, the flowers are usually in the trash and the vase is sitting next to the sink, waiting to be washed from all those soggy, smelly leaves.

Happy and excited?

"I know!"

"What?"

This time it's Shauly with the idea. "Mommy's *siddur* is really old, and the cover is not even attached any more. Let's buy her a new *siddur*."

A new *siddur*. Not a bad idea. Hmmm. In fact, maybe a very good idea . . .

I look around. Pinny's nodding, Faigy's drawing little pictures of *siddurim* on the paper in front of her, and Shauly has a big grin on his face.

"All in favor?"

Everyone raises their hands, including me.

"Signed and sealed," I say. "Mommy's birthday present this year will be a beautiful new *siddur*." I look around. Everyone's smiling, imagining how Mommy will love the gift. "So," I say brightly. "How much is everyone going to pitch in?"

Pinny reaches into his pocket and takes out a 50-pence piece. "How's that?"

I pick up the coin and toss it between my two hands. "This is not going to get us very far." I walk over to my desk and pick up a glass jar with smileys painted on it with special paint. My best friend Huvi gave it to me for Chanukah. I unscrew the lid and spill out the contents. Not bad, I think, as I count up all the money I've saved since then — my allowance, and also the money I get from Mrs. Cohen when I go help her fold laundry. "Seven pounds and 30 pence." I announce.

"Seven pounds and 80 pence," says Pinny, pointing to the 50 pence that he gave.

"C'mon, you must have more than that to give!"

"Okay, okay." Pinny runs to his bedroom and comes back a few minutes later with a bunch more coins. I count them carefully, and add the sum to what we've already got. "Eleven pounds and 93 pence. That's not enough! Come on, guys."

Faigy looks up from her coloring. "I don't have any money," she says. "But I can be in charge of the card."

I roll my eyes. "Fine. You do that. Shauly?"

Shauly gives a sigh, but he reaches deep into his trouser pocket and brings out a 5-pound note. My eyes grow wide. "Where d'you get that from?"

"I owed Shimmy 2 pounds, so I asked Daddy and he gave me this. He said I should keep it and the 3 pounds left would be my allowance for the next three weeks."

"Great!"

I put the 5-pound note into my jar and hand Shauly 2 pounds to repay his friend. Then I slide the coins off my desk into my hand and drop them into my money jar. They make a nice jangling sound as they hit the glass. "We're up to 14 pounds and 93 pence. Could anyone make it up to 15?" I ask. "Shauly?"

Shauly shrugs. He stands up and goes to his room, coming back with 7 pence, which he drops into the jar. Maybe I should have asked him for more, I think. "Fifteen pounds!" I announce. "Great! Now, who's going to come with me tomorrow to buy the *siddur*?"

Shauly, Pinny, and Faigy all want to come, but I think it would look suspicious, so I tell them to decide between themselves what they want to do and to let me know tomorrow after school.

This afternoon, Faigy's busy with one of her friends, so Shauly and Pinny both come along to choose Mommy's new *siddur*.

We head to Lehmann's, the *sefarim* store, and as we walk inside, Rabbi Raffles looks up and asks us what we want. "A *siddur* for my mother's birthday," Shauly answers.

I glare at him. I hate it when I'm in a store and the person in charge shows you exactly what you want. It takes all the fun out of it, 'cause then you can't wander up and down the aisles, looking and thinking. So I look daggers at Shauly, although he doesn't realize why. Rabbi Raffles takes us over to the *siddurim*.

"ArtScroll?" he asks.

Shauly nods and Rabbi Raffles takes down a *siddur* with crisp clean pages and a smooth brown leather cover. I take it and open the front cover. There, penciled in the top left hand corner is the price — £23.50.

I reach my hand into my pocket and finger my wallet. I don't have to take it out again to know how much is inside. Fifteen pounds. We're £8.50 short.

"Uh ... uh ... uh ..."

"What?"

"Uh ... we don't have 23 pound 50."

Rabbi Raffles looks at us and shakes his head. "Do you know that it's your lucky day. Apparently, we ordered far too many of these *siddurim* — there are many different types nowadays, you see, white and brown, and everyday and Shabbos and interlinear and different sizes — and we decided we could lower the price of this one. So we are taking the price down to £15."

"Wow! How amazing is that! That's exactly how much we've got," Shauly says quickly.

Rabbi Raffles raises an eyebrow. "Well I never. Should I wrap it for you, then?"

I think about the Hello Kitty wrapping paper at home that I saved from the beginning of the year when I had to wrap all my school books. Should I ...

"Yes, please," Shauly says, and Rabbi Raffles takes a large piece of silvery wrapping paper and carefully wraps the *siddur*. He even takes a small silver bow from under the desk. He's just about to stick it on to the corner when Shauly stops him.

"In the middle, please," he says.

Rabbi Raffles places the bow in the center and puts the gift into a bag for us.

"Have a good day, then," he says. "See you soon, and mazel tov on the birthday."

Today's the day! I race home from school to help Faigy put the finishing touches on a pretty pink card with butterflies all over it and to consult with Shauly about just when we should give Mommy the *siddur*.

"After supper," he says.

So after supper, when I've cleared away the dishes and we're all still hanging around the kitchen, Shauly clears his throat. "Mommy, we've got something to give you."

He takes out the *siddur* and hands it to her. Mommy takes off the wrapping taking care not to tear the silvery paper and her face breaks out in a huge smile.

"A new *siddur*. How perfectly beautiful. Thank you so much, *kinderlach*. This is truly something to treasure."

Well, I was happy and Shauly was happy and Mommy was happy. It had all worked out, down to the last penny.

P.S. Two days later, my father walked into Lehmann's, thinking that he would buy a spare *siddur* if the price was so reasonable. Rabbi Raffles shook his head. "Your children were very lucky, weren't they," he said. "The next day, we realized that we'd lowered the price too much and we raised it again."

So we had bought the *siddur* not a day too early or a day too late. Like Shauly says, how amazing is that!

My Story

Hello. My name is Dovy. I have brown hair and freckles. I have blue eyes like my mother. I am 14 years old. I am learning how to write in script. After school we have swimming or tennis and then I go to the store down the road and buy two cartons of milk and a package of ten rolls. Then I go home.

I like to play with my nephew. He kicks a ball and I stand in goal. One time, I heard him say to his Mommy (who is my sister), "You know, sometimes I forget that Dovy isn't just a regular boy." I was happy when he said that. I think it means that he likes to play with me.

When he has homework, I go back home and play.

I'm going to tell you three things that happened to me. Each time, I knew that Hashem is taking good care of me.

Number One:

This happened when I was a baby. My aunty was coming for lunch. When I was born, she gave me a bright red sweater. My Mommy didn't like it. She kept it in the drawer under my other clothes. But Aunty Rachel was coming, and she wanted to make Aunty Rachel feel good. She put the red sweater on me.

That was a good thing.

My brother opened the front door and took his bike outside. I wanted to know where he was going. I wanted to know what was outside the door. Maybe a fluffy cat. Maybe something else. I followed my brother out the door. I crawled through the garden. I sat on the sidewalk. I watched him cross the street and get on his bike and ride away. I crawled after him onto the street.

In the middle of the street there was a penny. It was shiny. I sat down and thought: Can I pick it up? I tried to pick it up and I saw that I could. It was flat. Some bits were smooth and some bits were bumpy.

Then I heard a loud noise. I looked up. In front of me, there was a car.

A daddy got out of the car. He picked me up and carried me to the sidewalk.

Then he knocked on a door. Mr. Schwartz opened the door. "Oh, that's Dovy," he said, and he showed the man our house.

The man knocked on our door. He told Mommy that I was in the middle of the street. Mommy started to cry.

"It's good your baby was wearing a red sweater," the man said.

"Oh my," said Mommy. "You're right. Thanks to Aunty Rachel."

See. I said Hashem was looking after me.

Number Two:

When I was 7, I fell down. There was a lot of blood on my knee. I went to the doctor and he sent me to the nurse. She cleaned my knee and put on a bandage. She told me to come back in two days. She would check my knee and change the bandages.

My Mommy took me back two days later. The nurse took off the bandage and cleaned my knee. It hurt a lot and I cried. She put on another bandage and told me to come back in three days.

When I went back, my knee looked different. There was no red. It wasn't wet. It wasn't sticky. It was brown and hard. A scab, the nurse said.

The nurse told me that the scab was dry blood, even though blood is always wet. The scab would protect my knee until new skin grew. When the skin was all ready, the scab would fall off. Hashem was making my body fix itself. The new skin grew under the scab.

Sometimes when I listen to music, the tune goes eh-eh-eh-eh-eh-eh-eh-eh-eh-eh-eh. Then I know the CD is scratched. It doesn't fix itself. But my body does. That's because Hashem wants us to be healthy.

When the scab fell off, the new skin was a bit shiny and pink.

Number Three:

This happened not so long ago. I was playing with a ball in the garden. I kicked the ball very hard. It went over the fence and into the street. Then it hit a boy who was walking down the street.

The boy looked strange. He didn't have any hair. But he did have earrings. I couldn't count how many because he kept moving from side to side and shouting. There were a lot, though. The boy was angry.

He pointed to his jacket and shouted and shouted.

Mommy came out of the house to see what was happening. She was scared of the boy. The boy started waving his hands in the air and stepping closer.

Mommy looked around. No one was on the street. No one could help her.

I would help her.

I walked up to the boy. "You like football?" I asked him.

"What?" he said.

"You like football?"

"Well, yeah."

"I play goalie. What do you play?"

"Uh. Also goalie."

I kicked the ball and he dived. He caught it and threw it back.

"Good." I said. "So you can be my friend?"

He looked at me and at Mommy. "Yeah," he said. "I'll be your friend."

"Good," I said, and I gave my new friend a hug.

He liked that. Then he pulled away and went walking up the street.

I saw that he was crying.

I think it was because he just wanted a friend.

Those are my three stories. I hope you enjoy them. New things happen to me every day.

Do they also happen to you?

Right on Time

I always thought I wanted a fancy watch for my bar mitzvah: I saw one in a catalog that had LED display, stopwatch, compass, and, if you go swimming in the sea, a button that shows the level of the water, and how deep you're swimming.

I wanted that watch really badly, until I happened to mention it to my Grandma. She told me to ask Grandpa to see his watch. When I did, I didn't want my fancy watch, anymore. I wanted one just like his.

"Come on, Shmuel, let's show you what a real watch is about," Grandpa said as he tapped a combination of numbers into his safe, turned the dial and the door swung open. He took his watch out of the safe and laid it on the table. When Grandpa nodded his permission, I lifted it in both hands, felt how heavy it was. Then I strapped it to my wrist, feeling the clunkiness. It was beautiful: heavy and gold, made with 17 jewels. It also had something special about it, maybe the history or maybe the fact that it had seen so many different people and places, and maybe secrets, too.

Grandpa showed me how it didn't work on batteries, but that there was a small knob on the side that needed to be wound each evening. Inside were delicate cogs and wheels, and they rotated, moving the hands of the watch and keeping it running on time.

The fancy LED watch went out the window, then. After all, I thought, in a few years time, there'll be even more features on watches, that will cost even less money. What I really wanted was a watch like Grandpa's.

"Why don't you wear it?" I asked him, after I'd looked at it and turned it over and tried it on and wound it up and held it to my ear to hear it tick.

He shrugged his shoulders. "For one thing, it's worth a lot of money."

That was obvious.

"It's precious to me. It was my grandfather's; he got it from my grandmother when they were *chasan* and *kallah*."

Well, I hadn't known that and that made the watch even more special. My name is Shmuel, and one of the people I'm named after is my great-great grandfather, the original owner of the watch.

"I think you should wear it," I told Grandpa. "I think your grandfather would have wanted you to enjoy it. He would have wanted to feel that the watch was being used."

Grandpa looked at me and laughed. "Maybe you're right," he said. He wound up the watch some more and strapped it to his wrist. "Maybe I'll get used to this."

From then on, the watch had pride of place on Grandpa's wrist. At night, he'd carefully take it off and place it on the nightstand next to his bed; the rest of the time it was on his wrist.

Grandpa is a very light sleeper, and one night a few

months' later, he woke up suddenly. The moon was shining through the window, casting shadows on the wall of the bedroom. As Grandpa lay there, his eyes open just a teeny bit, he noticed one of the shadows begin to move. It moved closer and closer to him, and then it reached out and grabbed the gold watch from the night table. Grandpa lay there, hardly daring to breath, until the shadow disappeared into the darkness.

"Were you scared, Grandpa?" I asked him the next day.

"Of course I was scared. In my mind, I was davening that the burglar wouldn't hurt us, that he wouldn't hurt Grandma. I pretended I was sleeping, and he just took what he wanted and went."

Then Grandpa told me something that he always said. "You see, Shmuel, when these things happen, you realize what's really important. It's not the gold watch and it's not the silver *leichter*. It's that we should be healthy and well."

I nodded. It was true and I knew that Grandpa believed it, especially when he made a *l'chaim* in shul to thank Hashem from saving him and Grandma from danger. But I was sad to say goodbye to that watch, and I know that Grandpa was, too. I also felt bad, like I was a teeny bit responsible for it being stolen. After all, I was the one who had suggested that Grandpa begin to wear it again.

The police never caught the thief, but the insurance company paid for some of the stolen property and Grandpa used it to buy a beautiful, much more expensive *leichter* for Grandma. She was happy with it, but she missed her old one: what's a *leichter* without some history? she said. The police tried to trace it, but, along with Grandpa's watch, it was gone.

A few weeks later, I was walking with Grandpa down the high street, where there are a lot of stores. It was cold and gray, and I wasn't surprised when it started raining. The rain came down harder and harder.

"Come, Shmuel," Grandpa headed into one of the stores. "Let me introduce you to one of my oldest friends."

Together, we headed into an old jewelry store that I had never noticed before. It was hidden between a dry cleaners and a deli, so maybe that explained it. Behind the counter was a man with white hair. He smiled at Grandpa. "I ordered the rain especially," he said, "just because I've been missing my old friends."

Grandpa took the man's two hands in his own and shook them up and down. He turned to me. "Shmuel," he said, "this is my friend Eliyahu Reich. We were in yeshivah together."

I nodded and smiled and shook hands, but inside, my heart sank. We'd be sitting here for hours now, I knew, while I listened to Grandpa and his friend talk about old times and catching up on all the family news. And for sure, Grandpa would tell Mr. Reich all about the burglary and how the antique gold watch he'd received from his grandfather had been stolen and I'd feel bad all over again.

I sat down on a stool in the corner, kind of looking at some of the watches with one eye, and keeping an eye on the rain situation with the other. I felt like the afternoon was dragging by, kind of like Grandpa's watch at the end of the day when it needs winding, and the hands turn slower and slower.

All of a sudden, the bell on the door jingled, and the door opened. The guy who walked in wasn't a kid, but he wasn't really a grown-up, either. He stood by the glass counter and reached into his jacket. He pulled out a watch and placed it in front of Mr. Reich. It was a gold watch. An old gold watch. Which wound up. I gasped. Grandpa's watch.

"I'd like to get this valued," he said.

Mr. Reich nodded slowly. "A family heirloom is it?"

"That's right."

Mr. Reich must have noticed the expression on Grandpa's face.

"I'll just take it out back to look at it more closely," he said and, before the guy could say no, he picked up the watch and walked into the little kitchenette. Then he picked up the phone and called the police.

Mr. Reich kept that guy distracted for a good 10 minutes, talking about the watch and about how to work out the value of different kinds of watches, and all the while, the kid was standing first on one foot and then on the other. I could see he was getting impatient.

Then, the door jingled again and three policemen burst through, each wielding a gun. The kid turned white and he put his hands up in the air. The policemen handcuffed him and searched him for weapons. They took him in the car to the police station and we were supposed to follow. So Mr. Reich closed his store, and the three of us got into his car and drove down to the station.

The policeman in charge there took down the file of our burglary and looked through it, nodding, a small smile on his lips. "Most stories don't end so happily," he said to Grandpa.

Mr. Reich smiled and nodded and patted Grandpa on the back. "It's good to be able to do a good turn for such an old friend."

"Well done on your quick thinking, sir," said the constable. He turned to Grandpa. "It looks like it's your lucky day."

Grandpa shook his head. "Luck has nothing to do with it," he said. He pointed upward. "Someone up there is making sure things happen just at the right time."

He's Right Over Here

I'm the oldest girl in my family, and my mother's the oldest girl in *her* family. So she tries not to give me too much responsibility — 'cause she remembers that it doesn't always feel good to be second-in-command. Still, there are some things that come along with being the oldest. I call them the *just jobs*. That's because they all go something like this:

"Oh, Yudit, will you *just* watch the baby for a few minutes while I put supper on."

"Yudit, will you *just* run to the store for a carton of milk."

"Yudit, will you *just* lay the Shabbos table."

I don't mind, not really, as long as I'm not in the middle of a very exciting book. Then I don't want to do anything except lie on my bed, leaning on my hands, my feet kicking together in the air, reading.

I do help out with the babysitting quite a lot, though. That's fine with me; my brothers and sisters are quite cute and they don't fight too much. One of the times when my mother always wants me to babysit is on Yom Kippur. I go to shul for *Kol Nidrei*, and also for most of the morning. By the afternoon, I'm quite tired and I'm happy to stay home. My mother usually puts the children to sleep, and then she goes to Ne'ilah. Just me and the baby are awake.

Even though I haven't been fasting for that long (I'm only just bas mitzvah, so I've fasted five fasts by now, including the three I did when I was 11), I'm really okay with it. Shivah Asar B'Tammuz is hard, because it's so long. By Yom Kippur, though, the days are much shorter and it's all over by 6:30. So it's like missing out on breakfast and lunch. And I eat so much on the day before (it's a mitzvah, my mother reminds me) that I don't get hungry until late morning.

My father says that the area where we live is "not very savory." That means it's a bit rough. There are scary people walking around, and quite a lot of drunks, too, especially in the evenings. So, when my mother goes out she tells me never, ever to open the front door. It doesn't matter who is knocking. That's one of the big rules in our house.

Anyway, now it's Yom Kippur afternoon, with that special kind of feeling that comes along with it. Mommy is wearing white, and I'm wearing a white blouse with my black skirt and there's the Shabbos tablecloth on the table and everything's a bit more quiet than usual maybe because there's no clunky shoe sounds or maybe just because it's Yom Kippur.

This morning, I was in shul and I davened and said *vidui*. I closed my eyes and asked Hashem to forgive me for the times I spoke *lashon hara* and argued with my sister and talked back to my parents. And I asked Him to seal us for a good year, where everyone is healthy and happy, especially my grandparents, who are getting quite old and weak.

This afternoon, I babysat for an hour so that Mommy could lie down and rest, and then I had a rest myself. After that, I felt a bit better, but now I see Mommy putting on her *sheitel* to go to shul I have this strange feeling and I know I don't want her to go.

"Anything the matter?" Mommy asks.

I shrug my shoulders. "No."

I crouch down on the floor so that the baby can climb into my lap and maybe even pull himself up on my shoulders. It's his new trick and I love to see his proud smile when he manages.

"Did you leave a bottle?" I say.

Mommy looks at me a bit strangely. "I'll fix one now. Are you sure that it's okay for me to leave? The boys aren't quite sleeping yet, although they're on the way."

I don't know what to say. The truth is that I really don't want Mommy to go. I want her to stay and daven here. As soon as I'm by myself in the house, it suddenly feels very quiet and then when the house makes noises, the pipes and the fridge and stuff, it gives me the creeps.

"Maybe you'll stay for another 5 minutes?"

"Sure, sweetheart." Mommy sits down on the couch and opens her Tehillim. She whispers for a while and turns a few pages and then looks up. "It looks like you don't want me to go to Ne'ilah."

I feel bad. I open my mouth and close it again. "It's not that I don't want you to go. It's just ..."

"What?"

"I'm nervous."

"Nervous?"

"Yup. It's so quiet around here when I'm by myself. It's creepy."

"Ahah." Mommy's quiet for a minute. "Do you want me to stay at home?"

"Uh ..."

She closes the Tehillim with a bang. "Don't worry, Yudit. I'm going to stay. I'll daven Ne'ilah right here, okay?"

"Okay."

I play with the baby for a few more minutes before I look up at my mother. "Uh ... Mommy?"

"Yes?"

"Thanks."

Mommy leans over and give my cheek a stroke.

Mommy flips through the *machzor* until she comes to Ne'ilah. Soon enough, she's standing up for *Shemoneh Esrei*. I give the baby a cracker and then I also stand up and begin to daven. I get a little shiver as I say the words *Chasmeinu l'chaim*. It's like ... c'mon Yudit, we're holding right at the end. We're almost by the *chasimah*. And when I take three steps back and bow and finish, I look up. Through the windows, I can see the sky growing that gorgeous deep shade that's halfway between blue and black. Yom Kippur is fading away.

I turn some pages in my *machzor* and begin with the *Avinu Malkeinus*. I say each of them slowly, trying to concentrate, asking Hashem to give us a year where nothing bad happens, no war, or illness, or plague ... or anything.

The last *Avinu Malkeinu* I sing softly to myself. Mommy hears me and she joins in. Our voices blend together and we sing again and again: *Avinu Malkeinu chaneinu va'aneinu ki ein banu ma'asim ...*

I see Mommy wiping a tear from her cheeks and I find that I'm also crying.

Together, we say *Shema Yisrael* and then out loud, like the *malachim*, *Baruch Shem ...*

And then there's *Hashem Hu HaElokim*. Our teacher taught us that we say it seven times because after Hashem has been so close to us during Elul and Rosh Hashanah and the Aseres Yemei Teshuvah, now, Yom Kippur is almost over and it's like Hashem is going back, separating from us by the seven Heavens. And when we say *Hashem Hu*

HaElokim, it's like we're saying, "Don't go! Hashem, please stay right over here with us."

"*Hashem Hu HaElokim*!"

Please Hashem, forgive us. Give us every berachah! I think as I say the words. *Stay with us! Right here, so we can be close to You and make You proud.*

Knock! Knock! Knock!

There's a loud banging on the door, and I open my eyes in surprise. Who could it be?

Knock! Knock! Knock!

Mommy wipes her cheeks with the back of her hand and, still holding her *machzor*, she goes to the front door. "Who is it?" she calls.

"It's Rabbi Schwartz! Please, open the door!"

Mommy opens the door. On the doorstep is Rabbi Schwartz, from the *shteibel* across the street.

"*Baruch Hashem, baruch Hashem* that you opened the door! You see, we've forgotten the shofar! That's right — we don't have a shofar! And we didn't know what to do. And then we thought of you and we all know how your husband has quite a few shofars, and you're one of the few houses inside the courtyard in the *shteibel's eiruv* so that we could carry a shofar from here to there."

My father is a *baal tokei'a* in one of the shuls, and he has quite a few spare shofars.

"Oh," my mother says, "well, we'll be happy to lend you a shofar. As a matter of fact, it's *hashgachah pratis* that I was home; usually I'm in shul for Ne'ilah and Yudit wouldn't have been allowed to answer the door."

Mommy shows the shofars to Rabbi Schwartz, who chooses one and hurries back to shul, to sound the final blast.

Mommy closes the door and opens the window. I shiver as the cold air comes into the room, and we stand, waiting. A few minutes pass and then we hear the sound of the shofar.

"L'shanah Haba'ah Birushalayim!"

Mommy closes the window and we start singing together. Yom Kippur is over. The shofar has been blown. But Hashem's right here with us.

Tefillah Triumph

What would school be like if the quiet kids were the popular ones? I think about that a lot. It just doesn't seem fair. The very first time teachers walk into the classroom, they look around and they know. And then the loud kids get all the attention: they get called on in class, they get asked question, sent on errands. They get put in charge of Rosh Chodesh activities and Chanukah *chagigahs*. The quiet kids, like me — I'm on the quiet side — we don't make too much noise or trouble. As long as we're scoring okay in quizzes, we're pretty much left on our own.

But that really isn't fair to us. Quiet kids also have things that we like and don't like. We have things that we're not so good at and things that we're great at. Sometimes, quiet kids find it hard to make friends.

Baruch Hashem, I have two good friends. But still, it's not nice to feel invisible.

I had been thinking about this a lot when our teacher Miss

Feiner announced a contest. "Tefillah Triumph," she called it. It was a good idea. Even though our class is small, with all the loud, talkative kids, davening wasn't exactly calm, quiet, and peaceful, which was how Miss Feiner said it should be. There were rustling pages, coughs, giggles, and some clown always davened at super speed, just so she could take three steps back and bow down for *Oseh shalom* while the rest of us had not yet reached *Modim*.

It was time for action. For a contest. We had to daven nicely for two whole weeks. And we each had to be the *chazzanit*, one time as well, leading the davening. Then, our names would be entered into a raffle. The winner of the raffle would receive a Tehillim and a fancy certificate with gold writing.

Davening time changed. No jokes. No shticks. No super-fast *Shemoneh Esreis*. Each day, our teacher chose someone else to be *chazzanit* and the girl would daven out loud in a clear voice. That way, everyone would know where we're up to and no one would get lost. When the *chazzanit* was done, our teacher would give a big smile, write the girl's name on a piece of paper and make a big thing out of folding up the piece of paper and placing it into a bag for the raffle.

In the meantime, I was nervous. I didn't want to be chosen as a *chazzanit*. I didn't know how I would ever have the courage to say the morning *berachos* or sing out the words of *Baruch She'amar.* Every time I thought about it my stomach would feel like it was fizzing and popping and I would feel sick.

But it was okay. Because on the day before the grand raffle I still had not been chosen. I had this whole mixture of feelings inside me: I was relieved that I didn't have to daven out loud, and I was maybe even a bit grateful that my teacher hadn't chosen me at all. But I also felt angry. The only girls who had not yet been entered into that raffle were Perry, who had davened *Birchos HaShachar* this morning, and Shuli, who was doing a nice job of *Pesukei DeZimrah*.

And as soon as davening was over, the two of them would also be entered into the drawing. I was the only girl in the class without even a chance of winning. Invisible again. And it wasn't fair. I was the girl who ALWAYS held her finger on the place. While everyone else had been whistling and giggling, I had been davening seriously, remembering what we had learned about standing before the King. I was really angry. Just because I wasn't one of those kids who made a loud noise every time they walked into the classroom.

We were in the middle of *Birchos Kerias Shema* that day when the teacher left the classroom. Every single pair of eyes watched her leave. She'd never, ever, ever done that before and I think everyone felt proud that she now trusted us. But she thought too much of us. 'Cause when everyone watched the door close behind her, they let their fingers slide off the place and their minds blank out. Then no one knew where we were. Even the *chazzanit*. She turned toward the back of the classroom and signaled with her hands — where are we? Girls shrugged their shoulders and made weird faces that said, "We don't know." No one knew what to do.

But I knew where we were — my finger hadn't moved. We were in the middle of *Ahavah Rabbah*. I leaned over to Shuli, the *chazzanit*, and caught her eye. I showed her my finger, glued to the right word. She smiled thank you and continued leading the davening: *v'sein b'libeinu binah lehavin ul'haskil* . . .

A minute later, the teacher came back inside and looked around. There was a smile on her face.

When we had davened *Shemoneh Esrei* and finished *Aleinu*, she made a little speech about how proud she was of us and that we finally understood what davening was about. That it wasn't about behaving well for a teacher, it was about standing in front of Hashem. And that's how she could even leave us in the middle of davening and come back and see that everyone had continued on so beautifully.

Then, she took out her gold marker and wrote down Shuli's and Perry's names. She folded the papers into crisp, neat folds and placed them into the bag.

"Looks like everyone has had a chance to be the *chazzanit*. Tomorrow we'll be drawing the grand raffle."

In my head, I told myself to stop being a baby and raise my hand and tell the teacher that no, not everyone in the class had had a chance to daven and no, not everyone's name was in the bag. But I didn't need to. Shuli raised her hand. "Uh ... Miss Feiner ... when ... when I was in the middle of davening, I lost the place. I was in the middle of *Ahavah Rabbah*. It was when you had walked out of the classroom." Everyone was listening to Shuli, 'cause it was very brave how she was telling Miss Feiner what really happened. Some of the girls looked a little mad, like they were scared that Miss Feiner would cancel the contest just 'cause of that.

But she didn't look so mad. She just said, "Ye-es," in that way of hers.

Shuli continued. "And I didn't know where to continue davening from and then Miriam leaned over and showed me the place."

I felt the teacher's eyes on me and I looked down at my desk. "Well done, Miriam," she said.

And then Aviva raised her hand. "And, Miss Feiner, Miriam hasn't been entered into the raffle yet."

"Has she not?" She looked down at the list on the side of her desk. "Well I never. You haven't been entered, have you?"

I shook my head.

"Well, if you helped out Shuli, you obviously know how to daven very well. I'll add your name now." Out came the gold pen again and she wrote down my name and added it to the bag. "You should have said something earlier."

I shrugged my shoulders. What should I have said: That the quiet kids are always invisible? As usual, I didn't say anything.

Inside, though, I still felt angry. Who needed Miss Feiner and her grand contests? That was how she judged whether or not a kid davened with *kavannah*? Hashem was the only One Who knew who was davening and who was day-dreaming. Real davening had nothing to do with how loud you could say each *berachah*, I knew. It was how much thought and heart you put into it.

The next morning, everyone davened beautifully, right from *Modeh Ani* until *Aleinu*. And then it was time for the prize draw.

I don't care what happens, I told myself. Winning means NOTHING. It definitely doesn't mean that the winner is the best davener. Of course, it would be nice to have the leather-bound Tehillim — and the certificate, too. But that's not what's important.

I told myself that, again and again, and scrunched my hands into tight fists to tell myself: Don't get upset.

Miss Feiner told us a story about *tefillah*: that there was a river in Brisk that was going to flood the town. And the Meshech Chochmah called all the children from *cheder* and they davened and Hashem made a miracle and the water receded. Then she reached deep into a bag and riffled around with her fingers. She pulled out a crumpled piece of paper. She opened it slowly. Then she looked up and everyone watched her eyes travel around the room. They stopped on . . . me.

"Miriam Koslow! Mazel tov! You're the winner!"

Everyone started clapping and cheering and I looked down at my desk. I could feel my cheeks turn red and hot. I was presented with the leather Tehillim and the certificate and I felt very, very special.

When I got home, I sat on my bed and opened the Tehillim. The pages were smooth and the cover made it look like it belonged to a princess. I said *kapitel* 130; we say it every day and it's one I know almost by heart. "*Hashem shim'a v'koli ...*"

Hashem listens to my voice, I read. Even though I'm on the quiet side.

Maya

Breathe Easy

"I just love your sweater."

My heart starts to thump. It's Dini. In my head, I call her Dini the Bully.

"Yeah, it would look just great on my baby sister."

I blush and look down, hoping that she's finished with me. She hasn't.

She peers into my face. "Are you feeling okay, Maya?" Her voice is sweet, sweet, sweet.

"You look a bit pale. You know, I think it would be the best thing for you if you just STAYED HOME."

Does she bully me? I don't know. She doesn't hit me or push me or flush my papers down the toilet. But, even without doing all that stuff, she makes me feel like an ant. Or maybe not an ant, 'cause an ant doesn't care what other ants think about him. I don't know *what* it makes me feel like, but it's not good.

What makes it worse is that no one stands up for me.

They're all a bit scared of Dini — she always has tons of friends around her and the latest stationery and she just acts like she's the big boss of the class. Or the queen. Maybe she is.

My class is full of girls who, when they started school, requested to be put with Dini. I don't know why I'm there. I don't belong.

My mother and teacher and aunts always ask me, "Who's your best friend?"

I tell them Talya, 'cause she's a quiet, gentle girl that I often sit next to. It's not really true though. Talya is nice, but she's not like a best friend. Someone who you talk to and feel comfortable with all the time. I've been to her house once or twice, but I wouldn't hang out there every Shabbos afternoon, the way you would with a best friend.

Talya once tried standing up for me to Dini, but the result was just terrible. The whole class surrounded the two of us and they were chanting this rhyme,

"Talya and Maya, together they stick

They're so good they make us sick, sick, sick."

We clutched hands and tried to stop ourselves from crying, but it didn't work. And then our homeroom teacher walked in and saw the scene and she told me and Talya to go to the bathroom to wash our faces and she yelled at the rest of the class. They had to stay in for recess for a whole entire week and they got letters home to their parents.

That only made them hate us more. And get more careful. So now, instead of chants and songs, there are horrible comments.

Some days are fine. Some days the girls are planning a party or something and they have other stuff to do. But some days I feel like I have a knot in my stomach the whole entire day. It only straightens out when I've been home for a while.

School's not all bad. The teachers are nice and the work is pretty easy. It's just Dini and her crowd.

I used to have these dreams that Dini and I got lost together in the forest. As we waited for someone to come and get us, I'd crack a joke and Dini would laugh and then we'd start talking and wouldn't be able to stop and by the time we got out of there, we would be best friends. Then I'd sail into school on Monday, tell Baila to please move because now I was sitting next to Dini, and all of a sudden I'd be one of the gang.

I don't have those dreams any more. If Dini asked me to be her best friend, I would run far away. Fast. Because I'm not jealous of her anymore. I feel sorry for her. And I feel very, very glad that I'm not a nasty, rotten bully like she is.

Mommy knows I'm having a hard time in school and she's trying to help me. She spoke to my teacher and to the principal and she was even going to speak to Dini's mother, but I stopped her and said that it would make things worse.

I asked my mother a thousand times to switch classes. But, the principal is very against it. She says that she prefers to work within the class and shift the dynamics. A person has to learn to cope with whatever situation life throws at them, she told me once as I sat with my mother in her office.

Well, that made me want to take the glass paperweight thingy that sits on her desk and throw it on the floor. 'Cause it's not true. I mean, what if she became the principal of a school where everyone hated her and all the teachers were mean to her. Wouldn't she look for a different job? So why did I have to stick it out in that mean, yucky class?

The whole summer I was hoping that the teachers would change their minds and let me switch over. Either that or that Dini would decide to transfer schools or move to another country.

It didn't happen. Come September, we were right back in the same classroom. I had a brand new schoolbag and a brand new pencil case, but it was the same old faces.

There was one difference, though. My new homeroom was on the ground floor and its windows looked out to a large, empty plot of land. For years, everyone's been wanting to buy it, but it belongs to the city and they have to decide who gets it. My school applied for the land to build a science wing on it, and a conservation group put in a request that it become a recycling center, and a kindergarten requested the land for a new building.

The kindergarten won. Construction started in September. Right opposite my homeroom.

It was fall, so our windows were kept wide open. Until the building began. Our air conditioner is the oldest and crankiest in the school — it makes a kind of whirring noise and the teacher has to put it all the way down to 16 degrees Celcius to feel a little bit cold. So Mrs. Scheiner usually just opened all the windows and told us to fill our lungs with fresh air.

The problem was, that when I started to fill my lungs with fresh air, it wasn't easy to breathe any more. My chest felt heavy, like an elastic band was wrapped around and around me and my breath got shorter. I put up my hand and Talya was told to accompany me to the nurse, who asked me if I have asthma or an inhaler. I shook my head, and then she phoned my mother and told her to take me straight to the doctor and when I get there to ask the nurse for a nebulizer.

After I used the nebulizer, I felt shaky and tired and I went to bed for the rest of the day. The doctor had given me two round inhalers. One was to prevent me getting wheezy, and the other one was to open my airways. I had to use them both twice a day, and the blue one again when my chest felt tight.

I went for a follow-up visit a couple of days later and the doctor listened to my breathing and he still wasn't happy. He gave me a different preventative, a stronger one this time, and started questioning me and my mother about triggers.

That meant reasons why I suddenly found it hard to breathe. Had I suddenly tried a new food? Did my mother use a new brand of washing powder? Had we just bought a cat or a rabbit?

I shrugged. I didn't really know what suddenly caused the wheezing.

A few days later, the itching started. I started scratching my arms and behind my ears. My hands too. Soon they were red and raw and my mother shook her head and took me back to the doctor.

Eczema, he said. He wrote out a prescription for a thick, yellowish cream to put on twice a day, an oily weird-smelling ointment to use instead of soap.

"There's obviously some allergic reaction going on here," he told my mother. "The sooner we find out what it is, the sooner Maya can be free of these symptoms." He looked at me. "Is there any particular place where you feel most wheezy?"

That was an easy question. "In school."

"So what's changed in school since last year?"

Nothing! I wanted to shout. Nothing, nothing, nothing.

Dini was still getting a kick out of teasing me and saying her clever comments. Nothing was different.

My mother rubbed her chin and looked at me. "You know," she said slowly, "this year there's some construction work going on next door."

"It's right opposite my homeroom."

The doctor sat back in his chair and swiveled from side to side. "Lots of dust?"

I nodded. "Loads."

"Well, there we have the culprit."

"Dust?"

The doctor nodded. "Dust is a very common trigger. The windows are kept open?"

I nodded. "Except for when it's really noisy. The air-conditioner doesn't really work.

"Well, I think that you've got to talk to the school and find a solution. This construction is affecting Maya's health."

My mother nodded and thanked the doctor, and we went home to plan what to do.

I was really quite nervous. I was already known as the kid who complains, which is really not fair because it really should have been that Dini was known as the kid who is mean.

And here we were, about to start on another round of complaining.

For this meeting, I didn't accompany my mother into the office. I don't know what my mother said or what the principal said or what happened.

When she was done, my mother knocked on the door of the classroom and asked permission for me to come out for a minute. Together, we walked out of the school gates and she put her arms around me.

"Maya, you are just not going to believe this."

"What?"

"I sat down and told Mrs. Hurwitz the problem and she gave a great big sigh and then do you know what she said?"

"No."

"She said that maybe the time had come for you to switch classes. The other fifth grade class is on the other side of the school. There's no dust there at all, they're not disturbed by the construction work. Starting from tomorrow, you can switch."

I gave my mother a big hug. I was so excited.

The next morning, I got to school early and walked into my new homeroom. I wasn't excited any more. I was just nervous. I'd heard that it was a nicer class, but who knew if I wouldn't end up sitting next to another Dini. I'm not the outgoing type, and I'm afraid that when I talk people are going to make fun of me.

But I didn't have to worry. The girls crowded around me, welcoming me, and a bunch of girls asked me to sit next to them. I was shy at first, but soon I began to realize that I could talk without worrying that my words were going to be copied and imitated and used against me. I slowly began to open up and I made friends with three girls who all have green eyes, like me. I haven't forgotten Talya, in my old class, but she says that she's happy for me. She even confided to me the reason why Dini doesn't start up with her — apparently, her father is Dini's father's boss! She is so scared of what will happen if she starts up with her. She's made a few friends as well, now.

And for me, now that I've changed classes I can breathe easy — in more ways than one.

A Caravan of Perfume

When my mother went into the hospital, she told us that she would be home that night. She was only going for a checkup, she said. But she didn't come home that night. I had to eat chicken — which I hate — and rice, which I don't mind, at my neighbor's house, the Goldsteins. I was embarrassed because in their family they don't have any older girls, only boys who are away in yeshivah. There was no one for me to talk to except for Mrs. Goldstein. I didn't really know what to say. We stayed there until after 9 o'clock, when Daddy came home without Mommy. My little brothers were already asleep, and he carried them over to our house, one by one, and settled them back in their own beds.

"Do you want to join me for a cup of tea?" he asked me when everyone was sleeping.

"Yes, please," I said.

Daddy made tea with two teaspoons of sugar and we both sat down on the couch. I was about to take a sip and

I realized that my tea was too hot so Daddy took it to the kitchen and spilled some out and added two ice cubes and then I sat and watched as they got smaller and smaller until they melted away.

Daddy yawned and leaned back in his chair and when I looked at him I suddenly realized that he looked quite tired. "When's Mommy coming home?" I asked.

Daddy shrugged his shoulders. "I don't know." He looked at me. "It might not be for a few weeks. It's going to be hard without Mommy home. You should know, though, that everything that happens is for the best."

I nodded, skipped up the stairs, and went to sleep.

It was hard after that, because Mommy didn't come home for weeks and weeks. We settled into this strange routine of going to my aunty's house after school and coming home later in the evening, when Daddy got home. But one day, I was playing ching chong with my cousins and it must have been early still because we hadn't had supper yet and my Daddy walked in the door. "Mazel tov!" he said. "You have a new brother!"

Wow! I was so excited. A new brother.

My father sat down at the table and my uncle came down from his office and wished all of us mazel tov and it was very exciting. There was one thing that was a bit worrying. Daddy said that the baby had to be taken to special care because he couldn't breathe by himself.

"But everything that happens is for the best," he told me.

A few days after that, Mommy came back from the hospital and we were so thrilled to see her. She hadn't been home in a really long time and we were all so happy. She sat on the couch with us while we talked and talked and I showed her how I was getting really good at jumping elastic, and my older sister just got back a *Chumash* quiz and she was showing that to Mommy.

"Where's the baby?" My younger brother, Yitzy, said.

The baby, Mommy explained, had to stay in the hospital. He wasn't allowed home and so Mommy was going to be spending a lot of time there. "Would you like to see a picture?" she said.

We all nodded. Yes, we would love to see.

So Mommy took out her camera and showed us a photo. The baby was tiny, smaller than a doll. He had tubes coming out of his nostrils and there were wires and things attached to him.

A few days later, the doctors decided that the baby would be better off in a larger hospital, which was about an hour away. Mommy and Daddy didn't really want to move him, because he was under the care of Dr. Johnson and they liked him and thought he was a good doctor. Also, the nurses were kind. Mommy and Daddy didn't want to start with a whole new medical team who might not be nice to them. When they said all this to Dr. Johnson, he laughed.

"You're in luck," he said. "Didn't you know that I'm also transferring there?"

Daddy and Mommy shook their heads. No, they hadn't known. But they felt happy that Dr. Johnson would still be there to take care of the baby and help them.

That was one of the times when we it was really, really clear how Hashem was taking care of us.

There was another time, too. After a few more weeks, the hospital decided that we could bring the baby home. Which was very exciting but it wasn't like . . . like other times we've had a new baby in the family. You see, the baby needed machines and monitors. He needed a tube with oxygen that would make sure he was breathing, and other stuff too. Someone had to watch him all day long, and all night, too. Someone who would understand how to work all the machines and watch the monitors to make sure the baby was safe.

That was a problem. The hospital gave some names and numbers of people who are trained to care for special babies, like ours, but everyone was busy. We didn't know what to do.

My aunt had an idea. She drove to an agency. That's a place where they find jobs for lots of workers. Most of the workers wanted to help elderly people. My aunty sat down to wait until it was her turn. While she was sitting there, she got to talking to someone. A woman who came from Hungary. She spoke English, but she had an accent and it was hard to understand what she was saying. She explained to my aunty that she had come over to England to get a job.

"Really? What kind of job?" asked my aunty.

"I could work as a carer," she said. "I hear that people are looking for people who will care for their elderly relatives."

My aunty nodded. She looked up at the number on the electronic display board. There was still quite a while until her turn came.

"What job did you have in Hungary?"

The lady was pleased to talk about her home. "In Hungary I work in a hospital. I was a nurse."

My aunt started to get the teeniest bit excited. "A nurse? In a hospital?"

"Yes, I work with the babies. You know, the babies that are born early. And the babies who have problems. It is a nice job but not enough money. That is why I come here."

"Well, this is amazing. I'm looking for a nurse who will care for my nephew. I need someone who will check on the monitors and change the air tube and things like that."

"Oh!" said the woman, "so it seems to me that ... how they say it? ... I am your lady."

My aunty gave the woman our address and told her that she would come and pick her up that evening, when she had packed her suitcase. The woman was very happy with the job and we were very, very, very happy that Hashem had sent us someone all the way from Hungary to help care for our baby.

⁂

Even though we were caring for our baby very well at home, he kept getting sick and going back into the hospital. After a few months, Hashem decided that the baby should be in a special place in Gan Eden, near Hashem. My Mommy and Daddy sat *shivah* and we were all very sad and there were a lot of people crying. Even now I feel sad when I think about it. Daddy and Mommy told me a lot of times that everything is for the good. That's the truth, even if sometimes we don't understand it.

Last week, my *parashah* teacher was telling us about Yosef HaTzaddik and how he was taken down to Mitzrayim. Most of the caravans that went down to Mitzrayim were smelly and yuck, she told us. The caravan that took Yosef was carrying perfumes and it smelled good.

My teacher explained that this teaches us that sometimes, something bad happens. Like, Yosef being sold to Mitzrayim was a harsh decree. But Hashem wanted to show Yosef that He decided how much he should suffer. And so, even though he had to suffer a lot, he didn't have to endure a yucky smell. And that showed him that Hashem was there with him, taking care of him all the time, making sure that he didn't suffer more than he had to.

I was thinking about that a lot and I thought that even though we had to suffer and it was very sad that our baby was *niftar*, Hashem still made amazing things happen that showed us how He was there with us all the time. Things like Dr. Johnson and the nurse from Hungary.

Yes, Hashem was there for us all the time. And He still is.

Hearing the "Click"

Everyone has a different head, my mother tells me. That doesn't just mean that they have different colored hair (mine is brown) and different colored eyes (brown, too). It means that they think in different ways.

Like my Aunt Raya. She's an artist. We have a huge picture on our wall that she painted. It's colorful and beautiful even though I'm not sure what it is a painting of. Not flowers. Not a sunset or the sea. (Sometimes it gives me a headache to look at it, but most times I like it.) She's very talented, but she tells us that she's not too organized. Like, she never makes lists. A few weeks before Pesach, she phones Mommy and asks her for all her Yom Tov lists — what to clean, what to buy, what to cook. "I think in pictures," she says. "And I *never* make lists."

I'm not an artist like Raya but I just borrowed a book from the library that teaches you how to draw cartoons. I'm practicing and I'm not bad, though I can't seem to get the hang of drawing noses. But I do make lists. So I guess I don't think in pictures.

But even though I think in lists, there are some times when it feels like my head really does work differently. Like when I'm sitting in class and the rebbi is teaching us Gemara.

I was okay at Mishnayos. I've got a good memory so I could memorize a lot and I understood them, too.

But Gemara is like another world.

I don't know if it's the language or that there are so many different things you have to hold in your head at the same time: a question, an answer, a proof, another opinion, a question on that opinion ... And my head is swirling.

I struggled all last year and then my father got me a tutor. I didn't feel so good about that. I never needed a tutor before and I felt like maybe I'm really not so smart. I always thought I was smart. Not the smartest, but regular smart. And I always heard it being said, again and again: You've got a good head on your shoulders.

But with Gemara, I was stumped.

My rebbi said that it would click and suddenly everything would make sense.

Well, it took more than a click. My rebbi had always told us to write the punctuation marks into the Gemara. I said that I have enough punctuation in English, so I didn't really tune in when he told us where to put commas and question marks. But my tutor sat next to me and took out his pen and made me do it.

He brought lots of different kinds of pens along and we made a key: yellow highlighter would be for the question of the Gemara, blue for the answers, red for important Rashis. I thought it was a bit babyish at first, but it really did work.

He also made me draw charts and write down questions, answers, and different opinions. It was hard work, but it made things clearer and easier to understand. And if we went to look at a Rosh or a Rif or a Ran, he made me put a marker on the exact place, so I wouldn't get distracted by all those hundreds of words on the page.

And you know what, rebbi was right (my tutor was, too). All of a sudden, I had that click! I understood what was going on. And it felt great.

That's not to say that it's not hard. It is. But all of a sudden, I've got my head around the way it works. I know that there's going to be a *kashya* and a *teretz* and different opinions and that they're going to bring proofs. And I know that if I write it down I'll be able to keep track.

I usually review what we've learned after Maariv, so I just use the Gemara in shul. But now we were going to have a quiz in school — on the whole entire *perek* of *Eilu Metzios*.

Our rebbi said that everyone who scored over 85 would be entered into a draw for a new wristwatch. I wanted the watch — of course, everyone did. But it wasn't just because of the watch that I wanted to do well. I wanted to show Tatty that I could do it. And my tutor. And I wanted to prove it to myself, as well.

So that night, after Maariv, I opened *Bava Metzia* and I started right at the beginning: *Eilu metzios shelo v'eilu chayav lehachriz*. The beginning was a little bit tricky, because when we had learned it in class, I wasn't yet in the swing of things. Tatty helped me, though, and I wrote down a few points. We had to go home after 20 minutes, though, because Mommy was waiting to serve supper. After supper it was already late and I had to go to sleep.

Just as my eyes were closing and I was feeling cosy and sleepy, I had an idea. I would get up early — really early, and have a chance to learn before Shacharis. I reached for my alarm clock and pressed it so that the numbers shone green. Then I set it for 5:15. I was going to sit and learn and pass that quiz with my highest score ever.

Beep beep beep! I opened one eye, then another, wondering why it was so dark outside. I looked at my clock. It was 5:15! Still nighttime. No wonder the house was quiet.

I washed *negel vasser* and tiptoed downstairs. I davened *berachos*, took a drink of water and opened Tatty's *Bava Metzia*. I sat and learned, reviewing my notes from *shiur* and from my tutor until I heard a cough. I looked up. There was Tatty and he was smiling. He patted me on the shoulder. "What a *masmid*," he said. "I'm so proud."

I was a bit embarrassed, but there wasn't much time to get to Shacharis, so I closed the Gemara and gave it a kiss, and ran to put on socks and shoes.

That evening, I told Tatty that I preferred to come straight home from Maariv. That way, I wouldn't have to stop my learning after 20 minutes. I could just continue on for an hour. Tatty was fine with that, so we ate supper earlier than usual and then I opened the Gemara.

I finished the *daf*, turned over, and I saw that there was a problem. There were pages missing — *daf dalet* and *daf hei.*

"Ta!" I called. "Look at this!"

Tatty came over and picked up the Gemara. He flipped through the pages a few times and then put the Gemara back on the table. "Printing error," he said. "I must have another *Bava Metzia* around here somewhere." He stood by the bookshelves and ran his finger across the spines of the *sefarim*. Finally, he shook his head. "I can't find one. How about you go over to the Staubers' and ask if they have a *Bava Metzia* to lend you?"

"Okay." Yoni Stauber is two years older than me, and he's a great kid.

Yoni was glad to lend me his *Bava Metzia*. "It was the first *mesechta* I got really into," he told me as he handed me the *sefer*. "Enjoy it."

I took the *sefer* home and opened it. I flipped through the first couple of pages, until I reached *daf dalet*, where my Gemara had skipped straight to *daf vav*. He had *daf dalet*, all right. I sat down and began to learn. It felt really good when I finally turned the page. Like, whoa, another *daf* learned and understood. When I looked at the next page, though, I noticed something strange. On the right hand side of the page, where *daf hei* should begin, was the first *amud* of *daf dalet*. *Daf dalet* had been printed twice. I turned the page. Phew. There was *daf hei*. But when I turned the page again, *daf hei* was printed for the second time. This was confusing.

The next page was *daf vav*, and then *daf zayin, ches,* and *tes*. Everything was in order after that. I checked right till the end of the *perek*.

But then I had a thought. I ran back over to the Staubers', holding Yoni's Gemara and my Gemara.

I knocked and Yoni opened. "Hey, Moishy. What's up?"

"Take a look at this!"

He led me inside to the dining room and I opened both Gemaras.

"See!" I showed him how my Gemara skipped *daf dalet* and *hei*. Then I showed him how in his Gemara, *daf dalet* and *hei* were printed twice.

"That is so cool!" Yoni said. He ran to fetch a pair of scissors and some scotch tape and sat down as he carefully cut out the two extra pages from his Gemara. He kissed them gently and then taped them into my Gemara. He did a really neat job, making sure there was no tape sticking out of the top and that the pages were 100 percent straight. Then he handed me back my Gemara, along with a little slap on my back.

"Seems like you deserve a complete Gemara," he said. "*Hatzlachah* in the *bechinah*."

My Gemara felt special after that, and I worked really hard to remember all the questions and answers of the Gemara.

A few days later, my rebbi handed back the test papers. I looked at mine. Ninety-seven percent!

"*Kol Hakavod,*" my rebbi had written in red ink across the top of the page.

I was thrilled. My highest mark until now had been 63!

I was given two tickets into the draw, but I didn't win. That was okay. I had an *even* better prize: my Gemara.

My ADD and My Opa

I had to be in a cast for six weeks when I broke my leg last summer. I had to wheel myself around in a wheelchair, with one leg sticking out in front. For a while, till I got oversized socks, you could even see my toes sticking out the end. Mommy sat me down. "Listen," she said. "You tell me what you want the next six weeks to look like."

"Huh?" I didn't know what she meant.

"Do you want to have a miserable time, thinking about all the things you can't do? Do you want to focus on your itchy leg? On how it hurts? If you do, then you'll have a miserable six weeks."

I watched her, still not quite sure what she was getting at.

"Or do you want to have a great six weeks? You'll have time to do different kind of stuff. Maybe you can learn photography or music or art or something you can do sitting down. You can catch up on your schoolwork, so when midterms roll around you're ready for them. There's loads of things you can do while you're in a cast — if you decide to.

"But it's a choice. It's up to you."

She turned to leave. "Let me know."

I thought Mommy was being very unfair — she wasn't the one stuck in cast. But after a while, I figured out what she was trying to say.

It's kind of like when they tell me that everything is *hashgachah pratis*. When they say that, they don't just mean whether or not you get chosen for the team. They mean where you're born, who your parents are, what you're good at and what you're really bad at.

All the background, all the raw materials, is what Hashem decides, they tell me often. You have to decide what you do with it.

The cast was itchy and uncomfortable but I stuck it out. I used that time to learn photography — first on my mother's camera and, after I got a brand-new one for my birthday, on my own. I never knew there was so much to learn about taking photos — one snap and you're done, I always thought. Turned out I was wrong.

Why was I telling you this? I get distracted very easily, you see, and sometimes (often, really) I lose track of where I'm heading. I have ADD, so sometimes my head's like in one place and then in another and then in another and I don't even realize I've switched. That's why photography's good for me. I focus, focus, focus on the photo. Flash! I've snapped the picture. And then I'm on to the next.

Oh, right. I was telling you how there's nothing we can do about the background of our lives. Like, I can't do anything about the fact I have ADD. I just have to accept it as part of my life, take my meds, see my coach, and make my choices. And I couldn't do anything about having a broken leg, either.

There's something that happened though, something in my family history, that I want to share with you.

And once I've shared it, I'll tell you why I want to share it (if I remember to, that is).

My grandfather — Opa — grew up in Germany. And there was a man who ruled Germany who was a big *rasha*. His name was Hitler, *yemach shemo*, and he killed a lot of Yidden. So, my great-grandparents could see that times were bad for the Yidden and they were getting worse and worse. First they just had to put a yellow armband on their clothing, with a *Magen David* on it and the word *JUDE (that's "Jew" in German)*. Then, Hitler said that no Germans were allowed to buy from their shoe store. Well, their customers were mostly Yidden, anyway, so it wasn't so bad for them. But there were people, my great-grandparents' friends, who had hat stores and clothing stores or who had printing factories and it was bad for them, and they didn't earn very much money anymore.

My great-grandparents decided then to send their children to England. They had some friends living there, the Seligmans, who promised to take care of them.

My Opa was the oldest brother, so he was put in charge of his two younger brothers as they sailed across the sea and landed in Liverpool. The ship docked and, shivering and scared, the three musketeers (that's what my Oma calls them when she tells over the story) stepped down into England. The Seligmans were at the immigration office, waiting.

Opa and his brothers collected their luggage and were ushered into the immigration office. It was stuffy in there and uncomfortable. They were given cups of tea but they didn't drink them because they weren't sure if they were kosher. Oma tells me that it's a good thing they didn't drink it, because Opa soon discovered that if there's one thing he can't stand it's English tea.

After waiting a very long time, the man at the desk looked

carefully at their German passports. The Seligmans were there, filling in forms and talking to officials, and although Opa was a bit nervous, he wasn't VERY nervous. At last, the man took out a big stamp and he stamped a passport. Then he stamped another one. He looked up and with his arms, he ushered them through the barrier toward the Seligmans. But there was a problem. As Opa tried to go through the barrier, he was stopped.

"No, no, no, young man. You're staying right here," the man said as he twisted his long, blonde mustache around his fingers.

"What do you mean?" said Opa. "Why?"

"Why can't he come with us?" asked the Seligmans.

"How old are you, buster?" said the official.

"Seventeen."

"Precisely. And don't you know that you're old enough to get a job and earn your wage? There are no free handouts in Britain, you know. You can't go anywhere until I have a guarantee that someone's going to give you a job. We can't have you German immigrants draining British resources."

Opa didn't really understand what was going on, but the Seligmans explained that his younger brothers were young enough to be in school, so as long as they had the Seligmans to give them food and a home, they were allowed into the country. But Opa was old enough to work. So he needed someone to guarantee him a job before he would be allowed in.

"B ... B ... But ... But now what?" Opa said and he started to cry.

The Seligmans were talking quietly between themselves all this time. They didn't have any simple answers, they said. Mr. Seligman was a tailor, he worked for a man who owned a store. He didn't have the power to give Opa a job. Who did? Who did?

Just then, a tall man with a well-cut suit walked into the office. He was clean-shaven, and he wore glasses and a gray hat. He looked at Opa, crying, and he looked at the Seligmans, who were whispering and wondering what to do.

"Is there a problem here?" he said.

The official explained the problem.

The man flipped open his wallet and took out a business card. He threw it on the table in front of the official. From where he was standing, Opa couldn't see the name, but underneath it said, Imports and Exports.

"I'll guarantee this boy a job," the man said.

He took out a gold pen and signed the papers with a flourish.

The official stamped Opa's passport and handed it back to him. Then he waved him through the barrier.

"Who ... Who are you?" the Seligmans started to ask the mysterious man.

The man walked a little bit ahead of them. He didn't answer. Just before he turned a corner, he looked back and tipped his hat. Then he disappeared. Opa never saw the man again.

So that's how Opa came to England and was saved from Hitler.

Now what has that got to do with me, you may ask. Well, that's part of the backdrop of my life, isn't it? It's like the color of my hair and where I live and the fact that I have ADD. It's even kind of like my broken leg that I decided to make the best of.

You see, it's only because my Opa was allowed into England and wasn't shipped on the express (if they have that) back to Germany that I'm alive. So that's a very big deal. It means that the background is highlighted in fluorescent yellow (like my coach tells me to use on my daily planner).

And there's for sure many other miracles that happened

to my great-grandparents and my great-great grandparents and my great-great-great grandparents and on and on. Like we say on Pesach, in every generation there have been enemies of the Yidden. So, in every generation, my ancestors survived those enemies. I don't know how. I don't know when. But it happened. And it even happened to my Opa. So the fact that I'm here today, to tell you this story, is only 'cause Hashem wants me here. He's made all those miracles happen so that I, Shimon Weiss, age 11, am here today to tell you an amazing story. I'm sure there are many more amazing stories just waiting to happen to Shimon Weiss, age 11. When they do, I'll be sure to tell you.

Cronk on Wheels

My parent's car is so old that it's amazing cars were even invented then. It's a 1988 Subaru, which means that it's over 20 years old. I've heard of people who put their cars into retirement after five years … but not my parents. And not this car. The doors squeak when you open them, and they tilt up at an angle. The air conditioner makes a lot of noise, but it only gets the front seats cool — everyone else sits there, sweaty and hot. Sometimes it stalls at traffic lights. Everyone is honking and beeping and the car just doesn't want to start. Mostly that happens with Mommy, not so much with Tatty.

But, as Tatty says, a car is a car and it gets us from A to B. And it means we don't have to take the bus, like some of my friends do. Also, I think that if we didn't have a car, we wouldn't get to do some of the fun things we do in that car. Or the interesting situations we find ourselves in. Like …

Like the time Tatty had to go to the city to deliver some

packages. He does that a lot for my Mommy's work — deliver files and packages and pick up paperwork. He offered me to come with him. It didn't sound so interesting, but if I went along, I would be rescued from bedtime.

"Please, Tatty, could I come with you?"

Tatty looked at Mommy and Mommy looked at Tatty and I could see that they really were thinking about it. "I'll keep you company in the car, Tatty." Then I turned to Mommy, "You don't like Tatty driving at night by himself, do you?"

"How do kids know just what to say?" Tatty mumbled, but he had a smile on his face.

Mommy rolled her eyes, leaned forward and messed up my hair, and pushed me gently in the direction of the front door. "Okay, then, Yedidya. As long as you've done your homework and reviewed your Mishnayos."

"Done."

"Then let's go, kid." Tatty put his arm around me and led me out the front door toward the car.

We got in, buckled up, and were off. There's no CD player in our car, not even a tape deck, so we have this portable stereo system that Tatty wired up to the cigarette lighter. We put on Schwekey, Tatty's favorite, and soon we were on the high road to Jerusalem, singing along at the top of our lungs.

It was a cold, dark, and rainy night. Even though it was fun helping Tatty pick up envelopes and deliver packages, sometime around 10 I started getting tired and shivery. The rain was picking up, too. It almost felt like last summer when we stood under a waterfall on a hike. Only then, it was like 100 degrees outside. Now it was cold.

"C'mon, Ta, let's go home."

"Just one more file to go."

Well, we delivered that file as quickly as we could, but it was dark and the roads were slippery. We had to drive really slowly. Soon enough we were out of the car, knocking on the door to deliver the file and hey, great, yippee, now we could be on our way home.

By that time, we'd listened to that Schwekey CD maybe five times and even Tatty was getting fed up with it. "Good that I've got you for company," he said, squeezing my arm. I wasn't so sure. I was thinking of my cozy, warm, dry bed and thinking that maybe bedtime sounded quite good, after all.

We drove through town and out onto the highway. There were hardly any other cars around. That wasn't surprising: it was almost midnight and the rain was coming down so fast you could hardly see anything in front of you. Just this great grey stream of water coming down from *Shamayim*.

Ba-boom!

Ba-boom!

The thunder started. I pressed my nose to the cold, wet glass of the window to see the lightning. In the dark, lightning looks incredible — bent and twisted and made of light that keeps on striking the earth. Of course, I know that it's really electricity jumping down to earth but sometimes it's fun to imagine things, isn't it.

There we were on the highway with the thunder and lightning and Tatty reached into his pocket and handed me his cell phone. "Mommy will be waiting up for us, and she'll be worried," he said. "Give her a call."

I unlocked the key pad and started dialing the number. But then there's this message on the screen: Battery Low, with a little picture of an empty battery. I dial the number anyway and Mommy picks up, "Hi Yedidya, I was just getting worried with this weather. I'll call you back."

I opened my mouth to say, no, don't call back, because there's not a lot of battery left, but Mommy had already put the phone down. We have a deal on our phone line, you see, that Mommy can call Tatty's cell phone for free, so Mommy always calls back so that the call doesn't cost anything.

Boy, was I relieved when that cell phone rang again. I didn't think it would.

I picked up, told Mommy we were on our way home, and then the phone went dead.

We drove for a minute or two more and then the engine started juddering. It made these noises: putt putt put putt, dajum, dajum, dajum.

"Uh, oh," said Tatty.

"Uh, oh," I said. Now the whole car started shaking. It wasn't really shaking, it was kind of rocking forward and back, lurching forward and then going back a bit. Kind of like someone shuckling during davening. But this was a car, not a davener. And it was after midnight. And we were on the highway. And it was raining so hard that we couldn't see anyone.

"Time to pull over!" Tatty put on his sing-song voice. That means he's worried.

We pulled over to the hard shoulder and Tatty put on the hazard lights. "Now what do we do?" I asked.

Tatty took the cell phone and tried phoning home.

Battery Low, were the words that kept appearing on the screen, along with this little beep, as if the phone had to show it meant business.

Tatty tossed the phone onto the dashboard.

"So what do we do now?" I said. I was hugging myself, running my hands on my arms to keep warm. Tatty looked at me. "At least I can turn up the heat."

That made the car a little bit warmer, but neither of us really knew what to do.

"I guess we're going to have to stay here until morning, and then we'll flag down a car to help us," Tatty said.

"You mean we're going to sleep in the car?"

"I don't see that we have much choice."

"But what about Mommy? She's going to be so worried!"

"I know. I'm hoping that she fell asleep after you spoke to her."

"If she didn't, maybe she'll call the police and they'll come and look for us."

Tatty gave a little shake of his head. "Let's hope that she just fell right asleep. In the meantime, there's one thing we can do that will help."

"What's that?"

"We can daven."

The heat was blowing on my face and making my eyes prickle but I nodded. Tatty said the words and I repeated after him: *Shir LaMaalos, Lamnatzei'ach, Shir HaMaalos, Michtam LeDavid* ... All the *perakim* you say when you're in trouble. We repeated them all twice. Then we said some other Tehillims we knew by heart. When we finished those, we moved on to the *Hallelukahs* from *Pesukei DeZimrah*. And then we sang the whole of *Hallel*, the two of us, out loud, and I did the harmony.

Just as we'd finished, we noticed a pair of red tail lights in front of us. Tatty made sure the doors were locked.

I heard a car door slam and then there was a tap on the window. It was a big man, wearing a furry hat and sporting a beard. He looked kind of old.

Tatty wound down the window.

"Are you in trouble?" the man said. His voice was deep and seemed like it came from down in his throat. He had an accent, but I didn't know where he was from.

"Our car broke down. Maybe we could borrow a cell phone and call a taxi."

Tatty put his hand into his pocket and brought out a 5-shekel coin. "I'll pay you for the call, of course."

"What is the problem?"

"Why, you a mechanic?"

The man laughed. "No, I work fixing sewing machines.

But many years ago, maybe 20, maybe more, I work in Russia fixing cars."

"You did?" Tatty asked. He couldn't believe his ears.

The man nodded. "This is Subaru, right?"

Tatty nodded.

"All the commissars have Subarus. Is the car I know how to fix bestest in the world."

He went over to his car and took out a tool box, then he opened our engine and, with Tatty standing beside him, shining the flashlight the man handed him, he started to work on the engine. I wanted to go out and see what was going on, but Tatty was scared I would get sick if I stayed outside in the rain and the cold. So I huddled in the front seat, wondering if the man would get our car started or not.

"They old cars but they good cars. Built to last."

The man grunted and tugged and pulled and tightened. After 20 minutes, he straightened up.

"Try the engine," he said.

Tatty opened the door and twisted the key. There was a sputter and a bang. Then, suddenly, the engine started to brum brum. The man kept it running for a few minutes to see if the juddering sounds returned, but they didn't.

"So now I will drive behind you for a few minutes to check that it works," the man said.

Tatty jumped in the car and pressed down on the gas and soon we were driving down the highway, the engine purring.

The man drove close by for the next 20 minutes or so, until we came to our turnoff. Then Tatty flashed the lights at him, once, twice, and I thought I saw him lift a hand in a wave as we turned off, toward home.

I was quiet for a while after that. I was thinking. "Do you think that was a *malach* or something?" I asked Tatty.

Tatty laughed. "He sure didn't look like a *malach*. I didn't notice any wings or any glow or anything." Tatty reached out and patted my arm. "But you're right, Yedidya. In a way he was a *malach*. He was a messenger, sent by Hashem to help us out of a difficult situation. There we were, getting so worried and even a little panicky. But Hashem had it all planned. And you know what?"

"What?"

"He always does."

Glossary

abba – father
Adon Olam – lit. Master of the World; prayer recited at the beginning of the morning service
Ahavah Rabbah – prayer recited right before *Shema Yisrael* of Shacharis
Aleinu – prayer recited at the conclusion of each of the daily prayers
amud – page
Aseres Yemei Teshuvah – the ten days of repentance from Rosh Hashanah to Yom Kippur
Avinu Malkeinu – lit. Our Father, our King; prayer recited during the ten days of repentance and on fast days

baal tokei'a – one who blows the shofar
bar mitzvah – the age at which a boy becomes obligated in mitzvos
baruch hashem – thank G-d
Baruch She'amar – prayer recited during the morning service
battim macher – one who makes the boxes that contain the parchments of the tefillin
becher – cup
bechinah – test
berachah – blessing
Birchos HaShachar – the blessings recited at the start of the morning prayers
Birchos Kerias Shema – the blessings recited before *Shema Yisrael* at Shacharis
bubby – grandmother

chagigah – celebratory party or performance
challah – braided loaves of bread used on Shabbos
chas v'shalom – G-d forbid
chasan – bridegroom

chasimah – the final signing or completion
Chasmeinu l'chaim – lit. seal us for life
chavrusas – partners in learning
chazzan – one who leads the services in shul; cantor
chazzanit – girl who leads the services in a classroom
cheder – elementary school
chizuk – encouragement
cholent – stew traditionally eaten at the Sabbath day meal
Chumash – Bible; the Five Books of Moses
chupah – canopy under which the marriage ceremony takes place

daf dalet – page four
daf hei – page five
daf vav – page six
derashah – discourse on a Torah topic
divrei Torah – Torah thoughts

eiruv – a halachic device that permits carrying in a certain area on Shabbos
emunah – faith
Eretz Yisrael – the Land of Israel
Erev Shabbos – the day before Shabbos; i.e. Friday

frum – religious; observant

Gemara – the Talmud

Haftarah – portion of Prophets read following the public Torah reading
Haggadah – the book that tells the story of the Exodus from Egypt
Hakadosh Baruch Hu – the Holy One, blessed is He
hakafos – circling around
Hallel – prayer of praise recited on festivals
Hashem Hu HaElokim – Hashem, He is the G-d
hashgachah pratis – Divine supervision and intervention on behalf of an individual
hatzlachah – success
heilige – holy

ima – mother

Kabbalas Shabbos – prayers recited on Friday evening, welcoming the Sabbath
kallah – bride
kaparah – atonement for sin
kapitel – chapter
kashya – question
kavannah – concentration in prayer or religious observance
Kiddush – blessing expressing the holiness of Shabbos and festivals
kinderlach – children
kittel – shroud-like garment
Klal Yisrael – the community of Israel
kol hakavod – congratulations
Kol Nidrei – prayer recited at the beginning of Yom Kippur
Kosel – the last remaining wall of the Temple Courtyard in Jerusalem
kugel – pudding

Lag BaOmer – a minor festival celebrated on the 33rd day of the Omer
lashon hara – evil speech
l'chaim – lit. to life; a traditional toast
leichter – candelabrum

Maariv – the evening prayer
machzor(im) – prayer book(s) used on Rosh Hashanah and Yom Kippur and festivals
Magen David – the six-pointed star of David
malach – angel; Divine messenger
Maoz Tzur – prayer (song) recited on Chanukah
mashgiach – spiritual guide in a yeshivah
masmid – one who studies with great diligence
mazel tov – congratulations
mesechta – tractate of Talmud
middos – character traits
Minchah – the afternoon prayer
minhagim – customs
Mishnah – statements of law based on teachings of the Tannaim
Mishnayos – the Mishnah as a whole
mitzvah – commandment

Modeh ani – prayer recited upon awakening in the morning
Modim – prayer of thanksgiving, part of *Shemoneh Esrei*
mussar – ethical teachings

negel vasser – water poured over the hands upon arising
Ne'ilah – final prayer recited on Yom Kippur
niftar – deceased; the deceased individual
nu – exclamation meaning "well...," or "so..."

Oseh Shalom – blessing for peace recited at the end of *Shemoneh Esrei*

parashah – the weekly Torah portion
pareve – food or utensils that are neither dairy nor meat
paroches – the curtain that hangs in front of the *aron kodesh*
parshiyos – the parchments within the tefillin, on which are inscribed certain verses of the Torah
payos – sidelocks
perek – chapter
Pesukei DeZimrah – section of Shacharis prayer containing praise of Hashem

rasha – evil person
rebbetzin – rabbi's wife
rebbi – teacher
rugelach – a type of pastry, consisting of dough rolled with cinnamon or chocolate

saba – grandfather
savta – grandmother
schnitzels – chicken cutlets
sefer, sefarim – book(s), usually on a Torah topic
Sefirah – the period between Pesach and Shavuos, when certain aspects of mourning are observed
Selichos – prayers for forgiveness recited from before Rosh Hashanah until Yom Kippur
seudah hamafsekes – last meal eaten before Yom Kippur (and Tishah B'Av)
Shacharis – the Morning Prayer service
shaliach tzibbur – representative of the congregation at prayer services

Shamayim – Heaven
sheitel – wig
Shema Yisrael – lit. Hear O Israel; prayer recited daily, a declaration of a Jew's faith in G-d
Shemoneh Esrei – prayer consisting of 18 blessings, recited 3 times a day
shivah – 7-day mourning period
shofar – ram's horn, blown on Rosh Hashanah and at the conclusion of Yom Kippur
Shoshanas Yaakov – prayer recited on Purim, after the Megillah is read
shteibel – small synagogue
shul – synagogue
siddur – prayer book
simanim – traditional foods eaten on Rosh Hashanah night in anticipation of a good, sweet year
sofer – one who writes Torah scrolls and mezuzos
succah – booth in which Jews dwell during Succos

tatty – father
tefillah – prayer
tefillin – phylacteries
Tehillim – the Book of Psalms
teretz – answer
tzedakah – charity
tzitzis – garment worn by Jewish men, with fringes at the four corners

upsheren – first haircut of a boy, usually on his third birthday or on Lag BaOmer prior to his third birthday

vidui – confession recited on Yom Kippur

Yamim Nora'im – High Holy Days
yarmulke – skullcap
yemach shemo – may his name be obliterated
Yidden – Jews
Yom Tov – holiday

zeidy – grandfather

This volume is part of
THE ARTSCROLL SERIES®
an ongoing project of
translations, commentaries and expositions
on Scripture, Mishnah, Talmud, Halachah,
liturgy, history, the classic Rabbinic writings,
biographies and thought.

For a brochure of current publications
visit your local Hebrew bookseller
or contact the publisher:

Mesorah Publications, ltd

4401 Second Avenue
Brooklyn, New York 11232
(718) 921-9000
www.artscroll.com